THE GREEN-EYED
Necklace

THE GREEN-EYED

Necklace

◆ THE REVOLUTION OF XERTA ◆

CHRIS WALKER

TATE PUBLISHING
AND ENTERPRISES, LLC

Published by Tate Publishing & Enterprises, LLC
127 E. Trade Center Terrace | Mustang, Oklahoma 73064 USA
1.888.361.9473 | www.tatepublishing.com

Tate Publishing is committed to excellence in the publishing industry. The company reflects the philosophy established by the founders, based on Psalm 68:11,
"The Lord gave the word and great was the company of those who published it."

Book design copyright © 2011 by Tate Publishing, LLC. All rights reserved.
Cover design by Kellie Vincent
Interior design by Blake Brasor

Published in the United States of America

ISBN: 978-1-61346-633-9
1. Fiction, Fantasy, General
2. Fiction, Action & Adventure
11.09.13

Introduction

Some years ago, a world called Xerta was hit by a force that caused humans,' animals,' and plants' DNA to be altered. Before this world was hit, wizardry existed and already had started a magical era. The object that hit this world was made of an element that molded the abilities of humans who were affected and gave them the name of mutants. Xerta was this world's name two centuries before tensions began between the societies that it consisted of. The inhabitants just referred to the world as *world*.

A revolution took place among mutants and wizards during the times the world was called Xerta. There was a founder of the element who traveled deep beneath the world's surface and gained control over the magical world. After conquering his power, he started a court system that consisted of a member for each continent the world had upon it. It so happened that this world had seven continents. Seven courts reigned with a certain power for each court. Within the courts, each member had a successor that kept the court blood within the family.

Tensions began to rise between the societies of the world, for they all strived for power. The start of all the commotion came from waiting for the chosen one to enter the battle between good and evil. The presence of the chosen one would hopefully end the chaos that entailed many wars and conflicts between the three governments that were formed: mortals, mutants, and wizards. For the chosen one to be found, it had to filter through many bloodlines from the founder of the element before the one battle was ended. The chosen one would be called *The Emerald Prince*.

Chapter One

It was midday, and the sun peered through the few clouds that layered the sky and cast upon the small town of Winnington. It was located in a valley between the Winfelton Mountains. The valley was huge. Long, rolling hills covered with luscious grasses and flowers and few trees plotted the land. Farmland filled most of the spaces around the city and outer parts of the residential areas. The environment just seemed really pleasant and peaceful. The day marked the two-hundred-year anniversary of the Battle for Sorcatum. All day long festivities and remembrance ceremonies were put on to celebrate the ones who were still alive and to recognize the ones who had passed during the battle. Many people from across the entire world came to join in and be a part of the event.

The town held many different cultures of residents since it was the home to the Mutant and Wizard Affairs Embassy. The embassy was created ten years prior to hold peace between the two magical societies: mutants and wizards. Two years prior to the creation of the embassy, harsh and unacceptable tensions began to arise, which led to it being built.

Mortals, in very little population, few wizards and witches, and the majority being mutants, found their homes in Winnington. Mutants found dominance in the two societies from their victory after the Battle for Sorcatum. With all of the situations still in the air, hundreds of people from each society across the world came and joined each other like they were all one. These people wanted peace; they were the ones who strived to work together to make the world better for all.

The president and founder of the embassy was George Winfield. He was a tall handsome man who wore glasses and had short brown hair. His eyes were the color of blue, and he resided in his newly built home with his wife, Jamie. They had been married for ten years and soon would be adding to their family. On the landmark day of Sorcatum during the noon hour, George sat in his office and conversed with his vice president to the embassy, Richard Manatar, about the major issues still coinciding within the three societies.

"George, you know today is a very important day to all of the people out here walking the streets. If we don't come up with some answers on how to fix the problems that are rising, your political image among all three societies might be in jeopardy."

"I'm not worried about my image and the importance of my career. This isn't the time to worry about ourselves. It's time to worry about the existence of an entire race and culture. There is no simple answer to any of the problems," said George, kind of taken aback.

The two looked at each other with non-settling glares, and both took a breath and sat silent as they looked out the window of George's top floor office. The window overlooked the entire grounds of the embassy, where many of the activities occurred.

"With only one Aeuradecore tree left, the courts' and very few witches' and wizards' wands are still able to connect and get energy from the core. The Fairydomins inform me that the abstraction from the core is not possible and that they must not try to force it anymore. It is causing too much interference with the energy transfer to even their weapons. There is also interference with the protection that we have given them."

"Must we call the elders to get perception that might help?" recommended Rich.

"That is our last resort. To do so we must be sure that is what we want to do. There is no letting them down on our part of the deal. Remember if we want something from them, we must promise much more," said George in a sad and uninspired voice. "We will do what must be done. That is final."

<hr />

The activities continued the rest of the day, and as the sun started to work its way down toward the west side of the mountains, people went back to their camps, and the night parties began.

The center grounds of the embassy filled with dancing and carnival rides that the mutants and wizards joined in to create from chairs and tables. They spun kids around in circles as if they were riding an actual ride. Friendly duels among witches and wizards who had wands were put on as a show and for enjoyment. The atmosphere seemed warm and joyful. Not a single person felt anger.

George was still in his office thinking about what to say to his people and how to even approach solving the still remaining problems that many witches and wizards of the sorcery community still experienced. His mind was scrambled, and he really had no idea what to do.

"Rich, come on, it is time," called George just a little after five o'clock.

Rich walked out of his office as George pulled out from under his desk a green-and-silver, crystal, rod-shaped component and glared at it. It was his wand—one of the most powerful wands to ever exist. He waved it toward the window that overlooked the grounds, and with a flash of green light, the glass and window frames twisted and transformed into a long walk-out platform that reached thirty feet out from the office. He got up out of his chair and walked onto the newly made platform, and Rich followed. When they stepped aboard, the platform detached from the side of the building and carried them out onto the grounds to greet everyone who had shown up.

George and Rich knew that this point in time was crucial for the existence of Wizardry and its people to still be able to live like they used to. Sorcerers used to roam the lands in small knit communities that held around one hundred people. It was not until Sorcatum hit when life as they knew it ended.

Horrifying images flooded the minds of all witches and wizards after the Battle for Sorcatum. It did not matter whether or not you lived then. It was a curse to all sorcery. The images flashed in George's mind and gave him motivation. He gathered himself and with anger and inspiration, he gave the best speech of his entire career. He didn't know how he did it, but as he finished his speech, he looked up into the sky at the sun, and as he did, he felt a chill go down his spine, and his entire body shivered. The signal finally came to him, and now he knew what must be done.

CHAPTER TWO

The wind started to blow as dark-black storm clouds rolled toward the little town of Winnington. When the clock struck six, Jamie Winfield began to start her daily chore of cooking dinner. As she set out to the kitchen, she noticed the sun was being blocked by storm clouds. Jamie wasn't the fondest of storms. She grew worried, noticing how dark the clouds were, so she went over to the TV and turned it to the local radar. Over the past hour, a huge mass of severe weather had grown over Serpent Lake, which was located about fifteen miles away from Winnington and got its name from being heavily populated with water snakes, and was heading toward the town. Snakes no longer populated the lake ever since a poison spill from a truck had made its way into the lake from where the truck crashed on the nearby highway.

Jamie and George had a nice-sized house. It was two stories high and built the previous year. It was Jamie's dream house, and it had everything she wanted in it.

Jamie, just remembering about dinner, went back to the kitchen and began to cook to get her mind off the storm. Jamie was awaiting her husband, George Winfield, to arrive home from work. As she cooked she noticed that the wind started to blow harder and that it had started to rain. When she was finished with dinner, she set the table with plates both for her and George. Jamie had to make two separate dinners; one was hers and the other George's. She cooked George a mushroom, gravy, and steak platter and cooked herself vegetable soup, along with a salad and pasta that she needed not only for herself but also for the twin babies she was pregnant with. Jamie was eight months along. She was having trouble getting around now since she was so big. The trouble usually came when she strained to get off the couch or out of bed.

Finally when the clock struck seven, Jamie saw headlights from George's car pulling up in the driveway. George pulled the car into the garage, and just as he pulled in all the way and the garage door began to close, a big gust of wind pulled off the door as it was closing.

George came bursting through the door that went out into the garage and began yelling. He knew the storm was not normal. His face was plastered with fear, and his body still shivered from earlier after his speech. He couldn't get the trembling to go away.

"Jamie, where are you? Get down into the basement and over into the bathroom. This one is bad."

He yelled the loudest Jamie had ever heard him yell. She sensed the agitation and worry in his voice.

"I'm over in the kitchen. I'm coming."

She dragged herself across the kitchen and over to the basement door as quickly as possible, dragging her feet. The weight she held up from being pregnant was just too much. When she reached the door to go down, the wind picked up and the house began to shake.

The black storm clouds poured down from the sky and encased the border of the yard surrounding the house like a circular box. At the top where the clouds circled, they enclosed and formed a bright red, orange, and yellow ball of light that emitted great amounts of energy.

Jamie hobbled down into the basement as George followed. When they reached the bottom of the stairs, they heard a loud roaring noise, and the pressure of the air became really unstable, causing their ears to go deaf briefly. The foundation and outer walls of the house all started to crack but not break.

George took hold of his wife and had to yell in her ear for her to hear him since the wind's roaring was so deafening, "This is it. They're here. Don't let this weaken you. Your powers might heal your body, but your mind must stay strong."

"What are you talking about? Nothing is going to happen. We're going to make it out of this!"

George wrapped his hand around Jamie's head, put it on his chest, and spoke the words Jamie always loved to hear him say, "I love you."

"I love you too," Jamie said while lifting her head to give him a kiss, but before she could the sound of the storm intensified and made their ears feel like they were going to explode again.

The swirling clouds that went around the house seemed like the center of a tornado. It was no tornado, though, but an attack scheme. The storm's eye, which was the ball of light, centered itself over George and Jamie's large, white home. Bolts of lightning came out of the blinding ball of light and began to strike the house. Each time a bolt hit the house, pieces of siding and wood shavings tore apart from the outer walls and were sent flying into the surrounding winds.

The Winfield home was putting up a great fight, but the raging storm had acquired forces that were just too much for the house to stand. George sensed that the house was about to break and collapse. He looked out from the bathroom and saw that the entire house was twisting and about to break off at the foundation. He clutched his wand from his back pocket and slashed it from behind his back and up toward the ceiling of the basement. At the same time the red, orange, and yellow ball of light sent a ray of energy down into the center of the house. The protective shield that George created only made it up along the walls of the first floor before the ray of energy hit it. When the ray and shield collided, a shock wave was created and caused the entire second floor to explode and scatter across the once-grass-covered yard.

George went back into the bathroom with Jamie and sat in there, waiting to see when the storm would stop. After a while it finally became calmer as the storm weakened a little. George went out to investigate to see if there was a way out. As he was walking out under the about-to collapse ceiling, he heard footsteps. He went over by the stairs and saw that the door had been torn off. There was a shadow forming every time lightning flashed outside, illuminating a figure in the doorway. Beyond the wall where the shadow formed, George could also see that there were embers falling from the sky. With caution, he slowly moved back into the bathroom at the end where the stairs once stood. As he made his way back, he tripped over a piece of the stairs that he didn't notice were there and fell back. When he landed he caused a noticeable ruckus. The stranger by the opening to the basement heard George fall and made its way into the opening.

The impostor had long, blonde hair, and its skin was the color blue. Blisters lined the cheek bones of its face, and where its ears were supposed to be only holes remained. The intruder then yelled across the upstairs to someone, "My King, they're over here." It was the voice of a woman.

The voice sounded familiar to George. And after one look at her, even behind the hideous torn skin, he noticed it was Rachelle Cavort, a once high-ranking agent to the Courts before she turned to the dark side of the war and began serving its leaders.

Above, George heard more footsteps coming across the upstairs floor; it sounded like there were at least four others. Rachelle jumped off the top of the steps and landed securely on the basement floor, and soon after, four others followed, with one of them still at the top of the steps. The hooded one at the top wore a long, black cloak and held a small object wrapped in a dark-maroon velvet blanket.

The strangers surrounding George were very disgusting looking, just like Rachelle. He noticed who they all were, though. One was a brown-haired man by the name of Lawrence Packel; another man with black hair was named Jon Robinson, and the other was a woman with brown hair and was named Abigail Miller. They all had discolored skin, like Rachelle, and long, knotted hair. Scars lined their faces as if they had been burned before; they had no ears as well, just the same holes in the side of their heads as Rachelle had. When they talked, it could be seen that their teeth were stained black and yellow as if they were rotting and could be putting off a terrible stench.

Not letting anyone see, George held the green-and-silver, crystal, rod-shaped wand behind his back.

"What do you want, traitors?" George demanded with a nervous voice, trying to sound brave.

"You know what we want, Winfield," Jon answered. After he spoke, mucous-colored saliva poured from his mouth.

"What? Get out of here now," George demanded, still trying to sound brave.

"Well, the thing is …" Jon said as he moved closer to George, " … we aren't going to leave until we get what we want. And if we don't get it, you will pay," Jon finished, standing in front of George.

George felt scared, so he whipped the green and silver wand, around from behind his back, and he pointed it at Jon and yelled, "Rebbelo!" A flash of green light shot out of the end of George's wand and hit him, causing him to fly back into the others. All of the others took out their wands from under their cloaks and pointed them at George. Their wands looked different from George's; they looked more like branches off a tree with small leaf buds perched around them.

"Give us the necklace, George, and everything will be all right," Rachelle said.

"Never! You'll have to kill me before that happens," George said.

"Well then, I can see that you won't give it up. And I shall grant you that wish."

Rachelle flicked her wand at George, and a bolt of red light shot from the end of it, but George blocked it from hitting him, causing the spell to hit the wall and shatter it. George leaped to try to run to Jamie so they could run for it, but he wasn't fast enough. All four shot a shockwave of red light from their wands at George, all hitting him, causing him to fall to the ground dead. George trembled no longer after what happened earlier after his speech. He lay there, drawing no more breaths. The intruders who were once a part of his allies had successfully killed the leader of the peace-keeping embassy.

Jamie was in the bathroom and knew enough not to say a word so she wouldn't get caught, but she just saw George die right in front of her. She couldn't hold it in, and she screamed at the top of her lungs. She got up and started off toward George to try to help him. She startled the four murderers, and they all pointed their wands at her. She didn't stop until Jon shot a blue light at her, which hit her and knocked her back into the wall. Jamie grew scared now because she landed on her stomach. She worried about her babies right away.

"Oh, look at this. It's Mrs. Winfield finally coming out to show herself," said Lawrence while walking over toward Jamie.

"No, don't hurt me. Please don't do anything to me," said Jamie while sobbing and holding her stomach. She had a terrible pain in her stomach.

"Oh, you'll be fine," Abigail told her.

"Shall we do it then?" Jon asked.

"Yes. Do it now," a weak man hissed. The voice came from what was wrapped in the blanket that the unknown stranger at the top of the stairs was holding.

The cloaked stranger at the top of the stairs jumped and floated down to where Jamie was. It put the small object onto the floor, still with the blanket on. Jamie noticed that the object was in the shape of a ball, and it started to roll back and forth very slowly.

Rachelle came over to Jamie and bent down. She lifted up Jamie's shirt and stuck a small knife into her stomach. She drained the blood gushing from the knife wound into a flask. When the flask was filled, she removed the knife from Jamie's stomach, and the wound instantly healed. Jamie's power of immortality had saved her.

Jamie was another kind of magical person. She was a mutant. She came from a mutant family, and George came from a wizard family. Their babies would be called mutant sorcerers. Mutant sorcerers could possess unimaginable powers that no one else in the magical world could. Both of the twins would have the power of a mutant and the power of a wizard. Mutant sorcerers were very rare around the entire world. The only known true mutant sorcerer was given the name King Falcort.

The other mutant sorcerers didn't posses the full potential of a mutant sorcerer like King Falcort. King Falcort could do extraordinary things when he was at his highest. He could move buildings with his mind. Falcort thought of himself as the paramount in society—highest of all; he should be like a god. With his self-loathing mindset, he began taking things from people such as their homes and land, and eventually their lives. After his fast-growing chain of terrible deeds, he started up his own army and turned even more evil. He became one of the best-known mass murderers. He got this fame after he killed tens of thousands of innocent wizards, mutants, and mortals. His army worshiped him in fear. If you left his army, you would be killed. Stay, and you would live.

To this point he was the best-known magical being alive. However, he was lying on the floor of the Winfield's basement inches from death and about to be brought back to his original state by Jamie Winfield herself.

Chapter Three

Jamie was lying on the floor, scared, and she didn't know what was going on. She tried to move to George to try to bring him back. In the middle of the floor, the small ball began to shake more, as if there was something inside of it. Jon had the flask of Jamie's blood in his hand, and he was stirring it around with his wand. As he was stirring it, he chanted some kind of spell, and the blood started to turn a blue color. It seemed the enchantment was starting to get harder to perform as Jon started to shake. Buds sprouted around the wooden wand and bloomed, and then a shiny blue string shot out of them and dipped down into the enchanted blood.

About a minute later, Jon yelled, "Healkedious," as he whipped his wand out of the flask, shattering it. The blood clung onto the buds of the wand and circled around the base. It formed into a long rod shape and glowed an even brighter blue than it already had been. Jon walked over to the blanket-covered ball in the middle of the floor and held his hand over where it lay. The blanket fell off the ball as Jon made the ball rise into the air. When the blanket fell off, it revealed a small crystal ball that had smoky contents with a weak red light shining from the center. Jon twisted his hand, and that motion made the solid substance that encased the contents of the ball to shatter. After the contents was let free, a shock wave of energy was sent through the room, causing them all to fall back a little and bend forward to try and stay afoot. The weak red light that was in the center grew larger and brighter as the smoky contents turned into a vacuum and started sucking air from all around.

The cloaks that all the intruders wore flapped toward the ball of red and the smoky substance that surrounded it. Soon the red, smoky contents began to swirl into the shape of a man, revealing only the shape, no facial features. Jon took his wand with the glowing blue rod of enchanted blood and forced it into the heart of the red-smoke figure. The rod stopped glowing blue and instead was ignited with fire. The shell of the rod cracked, and a reddish white light shined from inside of it. That same light began to flow through the red smoke like it was creating veins and arteries of a human and flowing through them.

As the enchanted blood shimmered and shined, the gray smoke that surrounded the red body-shaped smoke began to sink into the red-lit veins and arteries. As the smoke went into the crevices, it created the skin. The skin was charcoal black and in the form of crusty ashes. When all of the gray smoke had fully encased the body in the charcoal skin, the body seemed to start growing larger and forming defined features—the features of a man.

The small blanket that was below the newly made man arose from the floor, went around the man, and grew to a perfect size to cover the man's newly made body. His charcoal-burned skin separated and cracked as it glowed like the coals of a fire. And as he began to breathe, ashes poured from his mouth.

The four rotting-looking creatures, at least in Jamie's eyes since she had no idea who any of them were, gathered around the newly made man, King Falcort, and curtly bowed down to him. The four that were creature stricken aligned in a diamond shape around him while the cloaked stranger sat back by the wall next to the bathroom.

Jamie made her way over to George after she noticed the creatures had bowed down to King Falcort. The four figures that were bowing down to him were his only followers left to take care of him.

As the ashes poured from his mouth and fire bled from the cracks between his charcoal skin, the temperature of the room rose, and the heat could be seen radiating off Falcort. Jamie's eyesight was blurred from the radiation he was emitting. The floor beneath Falcort began to glow red from being heated, and soon after a streak of orange traced across the floor in the shape of a curvy *f*. The end of each tip of the *f* stopped where each of the four followers sat, bowing down in the diamond shape.

As Falcort made his way down to the ground and landed safely, he opened his eyes. His eyes looked like they were on fire but were glowing bright red and already looked human in contrast with the rest of his body.

As Falcort stood there, not able to move, the curvy *f* separated from its center into four rays of light. Each ray of light encased itself around the four followers like they were a snake squeezing its prey. The rays of light rose the four into the air, lifting them off their feet. The snake-like ray of light that encircled Rachelle carried her over in front of King Falcort and released her but still hovered around her waist.

"Rachelle, do you have the dagger?" King Falcort spoke in hoarse voice. And as he spoke, ashes poured from his mouth.

"Yes, my King. Here it is."

Rachelle fumbled around inside of her cloak and pulled out the dagger that Falcort sought after. The dagger was about two feet long, and its blade's edges were the color of ruby red. The rest of the blade shined silver and had a snake engraved upon it. The handle was ruby red as well and glimmered as Rachelle handed it to Falcort.

When Falcort grabbed a hold of the dagger, the power surge was immediate. The enchantment was complete when he got his weapon. After the connection was made, the red of the coals that made up Falcort's body, along with the red of the dagger began to shine such a blinding light that everyone had to close their eyes. As the light dimmed after a few moments, the charcoal skin had turned a pale white, and the cracks where the red coals were began to close. Black hair sprouted from the top of his head, and he grew eyebrows and eyelashes. But his eyes still glowed the defining red. As he held the dagger in his hand, he felt all his power return to him.

"Ten years is all that I have to stay in this body. Time mustn't be wasted," King Falcort said with a shake in his voice and paused. "You all have really helped me these past few years. And I thank you for that." Falcort raised the dagger up to chest high and held it in his right hand. He waved it at his four tarnished-looking followers.

The blades of the dagger flashed, and shot a wave of red light toward all the figures, causing their skin to return to normal color and their hair to normal length as what a normal person's would be. The figures looked normal instead of looking like such hideous creatures.

All of them began to thank their master, but he interrupted and said, "No, no time for saying thanks. I thanked you for taking care of me for only the past four years. The years before that, you stayed home, thinking I was gone and you were free. Well, those years ended when I was in need of someone to take care of me. I decided I needed five. Five whom I looked at as the best of the followers I had. One of them I already had at my side for the many years previous and still do today. But you other four I had to curse and use some of my only strength left to make you the ugliest creatures so you would be afraid to go out in public and would come to the only place that you were welcome: with me. So I rewarded you today with your normal bodies just like I have returned to mine. The important thing is that I wasted the rest of my power to call for your help, and it still took you four years to realize that it was me. It took so long that I had to send my only protector to find you and bring you to me. When he returned with my other four followers, I was inches from my death." King Falcort began to get angry now.

Falcort began to pace back and forth. "For all the years that you wasted of my life, there comes a penalty. Even though these past few years you were very helpful to me, there was only one who cared about me and was there for a reason. And the rest of you were only there to be protected." Falcort held his dagger up and ran his left hand down the blade. The blade twisted and formed into a long, red-crystal shaped wand that looked much like George's, except it was red instead of green. The shape of a snake coiled from the handle of the wand up onto the tip. The stranger in the black cloak got up and went over behind the doorway into the bathroom. "And for that I have no use for you at all!" King Falcort yelled. He raised his wand up into the air over his head. The rays of light that surrounded his followers leaped up from the ground, swirled as they formed into snakes, and tightened around each of them. Each snake sent shocks of energy through the four, causing them to plunge to their deaths.

All four followers' bodies crashed to the ground where the snakes had latched on, they burst into red flames as the evidence of their murder was destroyed. King Falcort looked at them as they burned. With evil raging through his veins, he looked over to where Jamie was and walked toward her. The stranger in the black cloak came out of the bathroom doorway and joined King Falcort.

"Are you ready, sir?" asked the figure in a deep voice.

"I am as ready as ever," King Falcort replied.

Jamie looked up and saw that they were headed toward her, and she grabbed George tightly because she thought this was the end of her life. Even though she was immortal, she knew that somehow her life as she knew it could end.

"No! Stay away from me!" screamed Jamie.

"Oh, don't worry. You'll be just fine," King Falcort said, smiling as he pointed his wand at Jamie's stomach.

The snake at the tip of the wand began to glow as a gold, shiny substance swirled around King Falcort's body and then twisted around his wand as the curse shot at Jamie's stomach. Jamie felt a surge of pain go through her whole body, and then she fainted.

King Falcort fell from all the energy it had taken from him to perform the curse. The man in the cloak grabbed him before he fell.

"Sir, are you all right?" the man in the black cloak asked.

There was no answer from King Falcort. The man in the cloak grabbed hold of King Falcort as tightly as he could until they burst into white flames and disappeared into thin air.

Jamie now lay there, unconscious, not recovering from the curse. She usually healed within moments.

CHAPTER FOUR

When King Falcort and his last of the once five followers disappeared, the wind stopped blowing outside, and
the clouds that were swirling around the Winfield home
lifted back into the sky. The dark-black storm clouds that
were above the whole city of Winnington had gone, and
rain clouds had taken their place. Lightning had stopped
flashing, and the thunder stopped rumbling. All was quiet
until the city fire trucks started up their sirens and set
out to find any survivors of the storm. Nevertheless the
fire trucks were not the first to reach the Winfield home.
Jamie's parents, Nelly and Charlie, were first to get there.
They drove up in their car, surveying the devastation.
Nelly jumped out of the car and ran up to the house to
try to find her daughter in the rubble. The front door of
the house was no longer there, but she entered where it

should have been. Charlie had gotten out of the car and followed his wife.

As Jamie's mother ran through the ruined home, she saw a glimpse of her daughter's shirt through a crack in the floor. She hurried over to where the stairs to the basement used to be and jumped down them to see her daughter lying in the middle of the floor, unconscious alongside George's dead body.

"Nelly! Is everything all right?" Charlie hollered across the now open level of the house.

"I don't know. I'm down in the basement, and Jamie isn't awake. George is ... It isn't good!" Nelly yelled back.

Charlie was down there in an instant, not even realizing the stairs were gone. He jumped and landed on his feet onto the basement floor.

"Charlie, she's never been like this before. She's always been awake after being hurt," Nelly said in a shaky voice.

Jamie got her mutation from both of her parents. Jamie's mother, Nelly, had the ability to move things with her mind, telekinesis. Her father, Charlie, had the ability to heal things back to their normal state just by touching them. The two genes combined when they had Jamie and created an immortal gene.

Charlie went over to George and felt his pulse. "Nelly, he's gone," Charlie said.

Nelly got up from where Jamie was and moved to George. The one thing Charlie could not do was bring back dead. He could only bring them back to perfect health when they were inches from death; they had to be alive. Charlie grabbed his wife, who was now crying, and comforted her. They were there, waiting for Jamie to come back to consciousness.

"Charlie, try to help her. She might just need some help," Nelly said, getting worried for Jamie's and the babies' lives.

Charlie got up onto his knees and put his hand just below Jamie's neck on her chest. He centered all of his attention on Jamie. Charlie closed his eyes, and in between his hand and Jamie's chest, a shiny blue light began to glow. Charlie began to glow blue as a silver substance began to swirl around him and down to his hand into Jamie. Charlie's whole body glowed silver soon after the silver substance swirled down into Jamie's chest and through her whole body. Charlie began to shake as he stopped glowing, and Jamie opened her eyes.

Nelly saw Jamie's eyes open and asked, "Oh, sweetheart, are you all right?"

Jamie sat up, even though she did not feel 100 percent, and replied, "Yeah, I'm fine."

Jamie got up to her feet and began to go into shock as she saw the destruction of her home. She fell back to the floor when she saw that George was lying on the floor, dead. She was hoping that all of this was a dream. Charlie and Nelly both held their daughter as she cried.

The emergency vehicles' and fire trucks' sirens grew louder as they headed toward the Winfields' destroyed home. When they arrived, they immediately found Jamie and her parents down in the basement with George's body. They immediately grabbed Jamie and put her into the emergency vehicle to take her to the hospital. The firefighters and rescue team took care of George's body. Nelly and Charlie headed off to the hospital after Jamie. When they arrived, Jamie went to the Emergency Room to have her babies checked and to make sure nothing bad had happened to her physically. They waited outside the room to await the news. And after a half an hour, they were told that the babies were fine and that Jamie should have a full recovery since there were no problems at all with her, not even a scratch.

CHAPTER FIVE

Jamie went home with her parents that night to stay with them for a while until everything was on track again. When they got home, Jamie asked her parents, "Did you guys see anything weird happening up at the house during the storm?"

Charlie answered her, "No, we couldn't see a thing. It was pitch black out, and we couldn't even see five feet in front of us during the storm."

"George was murdered!" Jamie blurted out.

Charlie and Nelly looked at Jamie as if they were surprised. "What are you talking about? George was killed during the storm," said Nelly.

Jamie told them the whole story about King Falcort coming to their house and killing George. She told them about the five intruders and that King Falcort murdered four of them because he was angry with them. She told them how King Falcort had been reborn and that he had his powers again.

"That's impossible. The Wizarding and Mutant Union told the whole world that he was killed and that there was not anything to worry about," said Charlie.

"It's been a long day. George always told me not to let anything like this make me weaker. He told me the day he died was the day I had to be the strongest. Moreover, you cannot even believe me that he was murdered. Why would I lie about my husband being murdered?" Jamie said. She was beginning to get frustrated and started to cry.

"Sweetheart, we never said we didn't believe you. I never believed for a second that King Falcort had been destroyed. However, the thing is, what did he want with George? Why would he have killed George?" Nelly asked.

"I don't know. But before I passed out, King Falcort came over to me and did something. When he did it, a surge of pain went through my whole body but mainly down in my stomach where the babies are. After that I have no idea what happened."

———

Jamie and her parents forgot about King Falcort as George's funeral approached and as the Winfield and Wincraff family came together. When the funeral ended, Jamie went to her insurance agent to meet and discuss all of her losses. Jamie received a half a million dollars through George's life insurance. She found out that George had a secret bank account that held a quarter of a million dollars. Jamie received a new house and car from the insurance company. She got about one million dollars' worth of replacement things after everything was said and done. Most of the money went toward the house, and she put almost fifty thousand in the bank for the twins. She would live with her parents until her new house was built, which would be a short time after she had her babies.

———◆———

Jamie's due date was in one week. She was very excited but very sad since George wouldn't be there to see his babies born. The next week went by really fast, and she headed in to the doctor after her water broke.

When they got to the hospital, Jamie was taken to the delivery room and had the babies within six hours. Jamie and George were keeping it a surprise until they had the twins to see what sex they were. When the first baby came out the doctor said, "It's a boy!" As Jamie pushed the other one out, the doctor said, once again, "It's a boy!"

Jamie gave birth to two very healthy baby boys that had no signs of any health problems or birth defects. Jamie was relieved. She was worried because of what King Falcort had done the night of George's death. Next it was time to see if the twins developed any mutant genes from their mother.

The doctors took blood samples from each and put them into a clear tube. If the tube turned blue after putting the chemical that checks for the mutant gene, then the babies would have or develop a mutant gene. As the doctor poured the chemical into the first baby's tube, whom Jamie named Franklin Charles Winfield, the blood turned blue. Franklin had or would have some sort of mutant gene. As the doctor poured the chemical into the next baby's tube, whom Jamie named Pete Arthur Winfield, the blood turned green.

This was very odd, since no person's blood turned the color green when the doctors checked to see if they had a mutant gene. The doctor tested the sample of the blood three more times with the same result each time.

After doing the test the fourth time, the doctor came over to Jamie and told her, "Well, the test seems to not be working. So the answer is that Pete will be a very unique child."

Jamie was ready to leave the hospital after being there for only ten hours. The babies were ready as well, and they seemed to have developed the same immortal gene as their mother since where the doctors got the sample of blood from had already healed. As they headed home, dark-black clouds were blowing across the city of Winnington just like the night when George died. When they arrived home, Jamie took the babies into the new room that Charlie had built for them and fed them. As she fed them for only the second time, she looked ahead and tried to plan the future for her sons but sensed that it was impossible for her to do.

Chapter Six

Months went by as Jamie began her journey into mother-hood. It was spring, and her house was half done. Jamie watched her babies as they grew and resembled more George than her. The twins started to walk when they were just six months old. She discovered that the babies would also be wizards. They were already starting to move things they wanted when they pointed at the objects, which happened to most young wizards. They would be mutant sorcerers, as she already knew. Fall came as she moved into her new house, and the twins' first birthday would be coming up in November. Jamie's new home was just like her last one. Time was flying since the day George was murdered. Jamie thought about him every night and wondered why King Falcort murdered him. She never went to anyone about King Falcort returning because no one would believe her even if she tried to tell someone. The only people who seemed to believe her were her parents.

As the twins' birthday came, it went by fast. Jamie still couldn't believe it was already a year since she had them. She bought them each a new tricycle so they could ride them around instead of playing on the swing set all day. She thought they needed various things to do, which by all means they did.

When Franklin got on his bike for the first time, he somehow made it float into the air like he was flying a plane. Pete, however, didn't seem to be showing as much wizardry as his brother, but he still showed some. Pete's real interest was fire. When Jamie was cooking dinner one day, Pete decided to get on a stool and touch the flame. When he touched it, the fire began to swirl around, making designs all over the room. Jamie came into the room and saw what was going on, grabbed Pete, and the fire went out. Though her sons were immortal, Jamie's motherly instinct prompted concern about them.

Another year went by, and the twins began to talk. In the past year, Jamie had gotten a job. She was working for the Winnington Police Department as a secretary. During her time working there, the twins stayed with their grandma Nelly. Jamie only worked there for another year until she decided she had enough money to last a couple of years until she would need to get another job. She wanted to stay home with her sons.

It had been two years since the night King Falcort had returned. Jamie was watching the mutant and wizard news show, only aired to special subscribers. On the show she heard them say that the new disasters that had been going on in Noldon and Ktyo might be related to King Falcort's followers seeking revenge for his destruction—which would be odd, due to his downfall occurring many years previous.

In Noldon, brand-new bridges were collapsing, and new apartments that were just built had been catching on fire, killing hundreds of mortals. Mortals were what the magical community calls humans with no magical abilities. In Ktyo one of the city's largest skyscrapers had collapsed, and the owners of the building were inside, along with hundreds of mortals.

No one knew exactly who or what made these disasters happen; they didn't even know for sure that they weren't accidents. What experts said was that the owners and some of the people living in the buildings were involved with King Falcort's army back ten years ago, before he was destroyed, and some of King Falcort's followers who survived might be out there trying to gather up some more followers to make a new army. Even though Falcort shunned out everyone that remained of his once prestigious army, these speculations still existed. The press would overtake any story and make it up just as long as they got money. Some other experts thought that King Falcort had a replacement and that person was trying to gather up an army. Though people speculated as to who was behind the attacks, Jamie already knew who it was.

CHAPTER SEVEN

Jamie took the twins over to her mom and dad's house for the day while she went to Winnington's news media source, having connections with the mutant and wizard news show, to tell them that King Falcort has returned and to let everyone be aware of the dangers that might be coming. She decided to do this after all of these years because she was tired of keeping it to only herself and her parents. She also couldn't bear seeing all the innocent people dying from something that could be avoided. The blood could be all on her hands if she were not to tell. She felt that the people there wouldn't believe her, but there was something that urged her to go forth with it, as if George was in her presence telling her to do so.

When Jamie got there, she went into the news building and went straight to the desk where the secretary was and said, "I have information on the new disasters that have been happening in Noldon and Ktyo."

"Oh! What is your name, please?"

Jamie stated her name.

"It will be just one moment. Let me page my boss," said the secretary.

Jamie sat down and waited until a large man came through a big black door that was in the back of the room. The man came over and introduced himself to her. His name was Mike Monroe.

"Hello, Mrs. Winfield. What kind of information do you have for me today?" asked Mike.

"Well, if it's okay, I prefer to go into your office to talk about it," Jamie said to Mike.

Mike took Jamie into to his office, grabbed a chair for her, and went around to the back of his desk and sat down.

"This is going to sound really crazy, but it's true, and I really hope you take it seriously." She paused and took a deep breath. "This happened two years ago, and you're going to wonder why I'm coming forward now when the attacks have already started." She sat up straighter and got into a more serious state of mind.

"Mrs. Winfield, whatever it is, I'm sure I can cope with it," Mike said to her with a warming and mind-settling look.

"Thank you. It all began the night of the storm two years ago when half the town was damaged."

"Our house was totally destroyed. We were down in the basement when George saw someone upstairs. I remember him tripping and causing a loud smacking noise. This is how they found us." She peered off toward the wall, admiring the painting Mike had on his office wall. "There were four down in the basement and one at the top of the stairs, holding what I believed at the time was just something in a blanket. The four *things* that were in the basement were the ugliest creatures that I had ever seen. They wanted something from George. But he wouldn't give whatever it was to them. So they killed him."

Jamie started to cry a little. "I ran out into the room to see if he was all right, but I already knew he was gone. I could see the life leave him after the flashes of red light hit him. One of the creatures sent a spell at me, causing me to fall. Then I became drowsy. Another creature came over to me and stabbed me in my stomach and drained some blood. But I'm an immortal mutant and healed right away.

"They were doing something with the blood as the one at the top of the stairs came down and set the object that had the blanket on and looked like the shape of a ball in the middle of the floor. The creature that had the blood turned it into a different color, causing it to cling onto his wand. He did something to the ball that lay in the middle of the floor, allowing the contents to flood out. It was very strange what happened next. The light coming from it was so bright." She paused again imagining the night very clear to herself. "And after that the small object became King Falcort. Then King Falcort killed four of the followers because he got mad. Then he came over to me and did something to me that made my whole body feel like I was being stabbed a million times at once, but mainly in my stomach," Jamie finished while looking at Mike's face. He looked very interested.

"Do you believe me?" Jamie asked.

"Yes. Yes, I actually do. You see, I have seen a lot of things in the magical world since I have been here in this business. When King Falcort all of a sudden disappeared fifteen years ago, I knew that he wasn't really gone. He was too powerful," Mike said. "He was brought back by using your blood as a healer and a curse that would allow him to be brought back to good health for only ten years. That is what I am assuming. And what he probably did to you had something to do with him taking your blood," Mike finished while Jamie looked at him relieved.

She wondered how Mike knew so much about how King Falcort could have returned.

"I will have this information sent to the press by morning. If you don't want, I won't give them your name. I will announce you as a witness. Does that sound fair?" asked Mike.

"Yes, that will work. I just want you to warn all the people in the world that he's back. And please don't say anything to anyone about me. I will let other people know when I want to," Jamie told Mike. "Well, thank you for your time and your support," Jamie said while she got up and left.

Jamie was watching the news the next day when her information that she told Mike became public. Mike kept his promise about not telling anyone about the information coming from her. But the information that Jamie gave about watching King Falcort return could not be proven. They had no evidence. All of the attacks stopped for a while, and Jamie knew King Falcort stopped so that he wouldn't be caught.

Chapter Eight

Three Years Later

During the next three years, Jamie paid no attention to King Falcort's return. There were attacks that she knew were put on by him, but she couldn't prove they were his work, so she kept quiet. She was at home for a while, taking care of her twin sons until they started preschool. Even though they were five now, their birthday came too late in the year to start their first year in real school. The preschool was for gifted children like the twins. The school was run by mutants and wizards. Jamie got her job back as a secretary. She was only at work until the twins got out of school.

One day after work, Jamie was on her way to pick up the twins from their last day of school when the sky all of a sudden got darker and a storm swiftly rolled in. When they got home, she started to make dinner while the twins played in their room. Jamie's babysitter was coming over to watch Franklin because Jamie had to take Pete to his little league baseball practice.

Franklin wasn't interested in sports; he just liked to stay home and watch TV. Jamie was fine with it. She just wanted him to be happy. It started to rain really hard as Jamie and Pete headed into practice. It also started to thunder and lightning out. It was a twenty-minute drive to the practice field. When they finally arrived, Pete's coach was outside, telling the parents that practice was canceled since the power had gone out. The team usually played inside on stormy days.

Jamie started home as she noticed the sky was getting darker. She got home as fast as she could, remembering the day that George died. When she turned into the driveway, she saw that her house's front door had been torn off and thrown into the yard. When she got up by the house, she raced to get out of the car.

"Pete, stay in the car!"

She raced up to her home to see what had happened. When she entered through the door opening, she found her babysitter on the floor, unconscious. She yelled for Franklin. Without hearing any answer, she began running down the hall to go upstairs when all of a sudden she was lifted from her feet and crashed into the wall. When she looked back, she saw a hooded figure coming toward her. Right away she knew it was King Falcort.

"What have you done?" screamed Jamie. "Where is Franklin?" Jamie demanded. Jamie got up and started over toward King Falcort with rage. As she started off toward him, he flicked his wand at her, causing her to collapse. She felt a loss of all her strength. She couldn't move.

He walked up to her and said with the same hiss in his voice as he did five years ago, "You never had a son named Franklin. You won't tell anyone about my coming here. You won't remember. Franklin will be fine. If you tell anyone about Franklin being taken, I will kill you." King Falcort spoke to her in a warning voice. After he said those words, a bolt of red light shot out of his wand and hit Jamie. When it hit her, she fell back and blacked out.

After King Falcort cursed Jamie, he went into the kitchen where Franklin had been when he arrived. King Falcort had performed a charm on Franklin that made him fall asleep. He went over to Franklin and picked him up. There was a flash of red flames where King Falcort was standing. Then he disappeared with Franklin in his arms.

When Jamie awoke, Pete was over her, saying her name, trying to wake her up. She immediately got up.

"Mommy, Mommy, where is Franklin?" asked Pete. Jamie had no recollection on how she got on the floor; she just knew that King Falcort had taken Franklin.

"What, Franklin isn't in here with the babysitter?" Jamie asked just to make sure she wasn't dreaming things.

"No, Lisa is on the floor, hurt. She won't wake up," Pete told Jamie.

Jamie got up and looked around the hall as she noticed that the pictures on the wall had broken. Then she saw Lisa, the babysitter, on the floor, unconscious. Jamie went over to Lisa and got her to wake up. Jamie called for Franklin, but he would not come. She started to panic since she saw that the door of the house was broken off.

After looking around the house, she remembered King Falcort's words about not telling anyone about Franklin or else he would kill her.

She looked toward Lisa and told her, "Go home. It isn't safe here." Lisa listened to Jamie's instructions and left. Lisa was in a state of total bewilderment.

Jamie didn't know what to do. She thought of calling the police. *But what good would that do?* she thought. King Falcort was way more powerful than they were. She grabbed Pete and took him into his room. "Stay in here. I'll be right back, honey."

She decided to call her parents and tell them what had happened. When her mother picked up, Jamie said to her, "He has taken Franklin ... King Falcort has taken Franklin." She began to cry after she told her mother.

"What? Why in the world would he take Franklin?" Nelly questioned in a nervous voice.

"I don't know. I'm not supposed to tell anyone. He said he would kill me," Jamie cried.

"What? He can't kill you, you're immortal," Nelly said in a confident voice.

Nelly began to say something else but was stopped by King Falcort's voice saying, "I told you not to tell anyone." Jamie dropped the phone, and it fell to the ground and broke.

In the middle of the room was a flash of red flames as King Falcort emerged out of them with Franklin still in his arms.

"I told you not to tell anyone. Franklin will be just fine. Now, don't worry about anything. If you tell another soul, I will kill you along with your parents," King Falcort said while he flicked his wand at Jamie once again.

Pain went through Jamie's whole body. Cuts were spurting blood all over her. She felt like she was going to explode. Then King Falcort lowered his wand, and the pain went away.

"Now, that is just a taste of what it will feel like if you tell anyone else," King Falcort warned her as he vanished within the flash of red flames.

Jamie fell to the floor, crying, as all the cuts on her body healed. She was crying for her son's life, her family's, and for hers. She never told anyone again, and her parents didn't either. Jamie believed King Falcort about Franklin being fine. But that was one of the many mistakes Jamie and her family would make.

CHAPTER NINE

Ten Years Later

Jamie was always a weaker person even though she was immortal. Jamie, along with her parents, wasn't the smartest or brightest person either; George was always the tough one when it came to hard times. Jamie never told a soul about Franklin except her parents. Her parents never told anyone either for the sake of staying alive. A normal being would sacrifice their own life for a loved one, but fear came over Jamie and her parents of dying. They only hoped for the best.

As Pete grew older, he soon forgot about his brother who was kidnapped when they were five. Jamie never mentioned anything to him since the incident happened. Pete was fifteen years old now and had no control of his power. It wasn't like when he was little. Then he could move things without trying. It was very hard for him to do anything that had to do with magic. The reason for the trouble with his powers was the mutant gene. The wizard powers he possessed were more mature now and needed more experience before they would be at full potential. He needed a wand to possess all his wizard powers, and he also needed to discover his other mutant powers except the immortal one to be able to control them fully.

Mutant sorcerers usually had multiple mutant genes since they also had wizard powers. The wizard powers gave them extra mutant genes. Pete knew he had other powers but hadn't discovered them yet. It was very hard for him to discover them since he had no control over them.

Pete loved life as it was until his mother started dating. Jamie started to date this guy named Mark Jansen. Mark had a son named Drandon. Pete and Drandon never got along. Drandon was really mean to Pete and would always push him down and punch him in the arm. Even though it wouldn't hurt him, it was still annoying. Pete and Jamie decided not to tell Mark and Drandon anything about them being mutants and about Pete also being a wizard. Jamie didn't want Mark to run off because this was the first guy she actually liked since George died. Jamie and Mark were dating for six months when they decided to move in together. Mark and Drandon were going to move in with Pete and Jamie. Pete disliked the idea very much because he knew he would hurt Drandon in some way when he finally exploded on him, but Jamie wasn't worried about it; she just told Pete to keep his temper under control.

When Mark and Drandon moved in, Pete was forced to share a room with Drandon. Pete hated that idea even more than having them move in, so he decided to build himself a room in the basement. Pete wasn't in the basement much but decided that it was the best spot for him to get away from Drandon. So he went down into one of the rooms coming off the main room of the basement and decided that it would be his new room. He made sure it was all right with his mom first. The only thing Pete liked about the room was that it contained all of his dad's old stuff. Pete was curious to see what kind of wizard his dad was.

Pete got a new bed after he cleaned out part of the room. And he slept in there every night. There was a shelf on the wall that contained his dad's belongings and an old pot that had a cool design on it that Pete liked, so he kept it.

Pete was going to a public school in Winnington but soon would be going to a school called Goodrick's School of Mutant and Wizard Sorcery. There he would be able to learn how to control his mutant powers and learn about wizardry. The school was located in the middle of nowhere; no one knew where it was except a few people, and it had to be somewhere where mortals wouldn't be able to find it. Pete wouldn't be going there for another couple of months until this school year ended.

The school was among what the magical world called their secret colony. In the colony, which was named the Xertan Colony, there were many businesses that circulated with the magical community's economy. The Xertan Colony was an island about half the size of New York City and was mainly layered with forest and water. The outer parts of the colony had mountains lining it to help keep outsiders out as well. The entrance to the colony was through, surprisingly, Goodrick's school. The reason for this was because the school had the best security measures.

Pete was very excited about going to his new school. He didn't like his current school because he couldn't express himself by using his powers. Pete didn't have a lot of friends; he didn't really like anyone because they all thought he was too smart. They all thought he was weird for being smarter than them. Pete always got As on his papers and never answered a question wrong when the teacher asked him one. He had over one hundred percent in every class, and no one liked him for that.

Pete liked to do a lot of things. He barely even tried in school; he never studied. Instead he played with fire, swam, and jumped off the top of trees. Pete could do a lot of things because whenever he would get hurt; he would heal within seconds.

When Pete was in his room playing on his computer one night, he decided to look through some of his dad's old stuff. He went over to the shelf and grabbed an old scrapbook and opened it. Inside were pictures of his dad and his mother back before he was born. He put that book back and noticed a box on top of the shelf that said George Winfield on it. He decided to climb up the shelf to the box and grab it. As he started to climb, he was just about to the box when his foot hit the pot with the cool design on it. The pot slid to the edge of the shelf, teetered briefly, and careened downward. When it hit the floor, the top fell off, and the pot broke into a hundred pieces. A black dirt-and-sand mixture spread over the floor. Within the shattered pieces of glass and the black-dirt-and-sand mixture, something shiny caught Pete's eye. The silver necklace with a green eye in the middle seemed to grab Pete's mind as if it was a part of him, as if it needed him, as if this moment wasn't an accident.

Chapter Ten

Pete immediately jumped to the floor to find his dad's possessions scattered everywhere. But all of his attention was turned from his guilt to the necklace on the floor. Pete bent down and picked it up. As soon as he touched it, the green eye in the middle began to glow.

Pete felt a jolt of pain shoot through his body, causing him to lose all his strength, which caused him to fall to the floor. As he fell, his hand gripped the necklace. When he hit the floor, images of people started going through his mind. All he could see were the pictures with a green haze surrounding them. Pete had no idea what had happened. He was swirling around in a tunnel surrounded by green fire. Pete felt his strength coming back as he swirled around the tunnel that now was coming to nothing but a haze. He was being carried very fast away from the tunnel as he fell down into this small little room that had book-shelves covering the walls.

Pete lay face down on the floor of the little room. As he got up, he soon noticed a man was sitting in front of him in a chair, the same chair that his mother had inside their family room. Pete immediately noticed that the man resembled him a lot. Pete's first thought was that the man was his father. And it was. The room Pete was in didn't seem like he was actually there. It appeared to be some kind of memory.

As Pete sat there and looked at his father, George began to say something. "I don't know who is seeing this right now. Whoever you are, you are probably wondering where you are and what this is. This is a part of my soul that I have locked into the necklace to explain to the person who finds it about all of its powers. This necklace cannot be used by evil after I have used it. It shall only go to one of my descendents, which my wife and I are expecting here in a few months. This necklace has powers that are unimaginable. If evil were to get a hold of this after one of my descendents, the world could come to an end. The power the necklace holds will soon be shown to you. I will help you use the powers that are in the necklace so you can defeat evil." George wasn't speaking to Pete like a normal person would; it was like he was talking to the air. "Since you have now found this, you are capable of controlling the world. But don't let the power overcome you, or you shall be controlled by the power," George finished as the entire room began to swirl and Pete was taken back to his original state of mind back in his room.

When Pete opened his eyes, they were glowing the same green color as the necklace. Pete felt a sense of triumph come over him. For once in his life, he had discovered something that his mom didn't already know about. He had found a part of his father's soul locked in an old necklace. Pete got up with the necklace still in his hand. He put the necklace on, and when he did, the chain tightened around his neck. Pete quickly grabbed for it when it did that, but it was all right. It didn't tighten too much.

Pete decided that he wasn't going to tell anyone about what had happened that night. He decided that it would be his own little secret. It was the only connection he had with his father. The only thing his mom had told him about his dad was that he had died in a car crash before Pete was even born.

The next day Pete decided to go for a walk out back in the woods. Walks were one of his favorite things to do. It was winter, and there was a foot of snow on the ground. It had snowed for the past three days, but today the sun was shining. As he was walking down a trail that went back into a field behind his house, he began to lose his strength again. But this time he was being controlled by something else. His whole body was engulfed in green fire as his hands rose into the air. Snow began to blow back toward his house like a huge cloud. Then he remembered what his father had said: *Control the power, or the power will control you.* And with that thought, Pete centered all of his attention on stopping the snow from blowing. Pete had surges of pain shocking him throughout his whole body like lightning was striking him.

Pete saw the snow fall as he fell to the ground and blacked out. He was in the green haze again as his father came back into the picture. George told Pete, "You are hearing this now because you have controlled the power for the first time. The more you do this, the easier it will be to control." As his father disappeared, Pete awoke. *All of this seems like a game.*

Chapter Eleven

When Pete got back up to the house, he saw that all the snow that he sent toward the house was all over the place. Drifts had formed everywhere, and snow was on everything.

When he got into the house, his mother met him, and as soon as he opened the door, she asked him, "Are you all right?"

"Yeah, I'm fine, Mom," Pete told her.

"I was worried that something might have happened to you out there. The storm had come in at like a hundred miles an hour," Jamie said with a shaky voice.

"Mom, you know nothing can really hurt me. I'm immortal just like you," Pete told her sarcastically.

"I know. It's just that I worry about things like this. I worry about you," Jamie told Pete in a soft, caring voice.

Pete came into the house and went upstairs to get a shower. Drandon met him up there.

"Gosh, Pete, about gave your mom a heart attack," Drandon said, all the while punching him in the arm.

"Knock it off, Drandon. She was fine," Pete said while pushing Drandon away.

"Don't push me!" Drandon said with rage in his eyes as he knocked Pete down.

Pete felt the power of the necklace erupt in him as the necklace began to glow under his shirt. Pete couldn't control the rage that had erupted. He lay on the ground, watching the blast of green light shoot out from the end of his hands and hit Drandon. He couldn't control it; it happened too fast.

As the blast of green light hit Drandon, he flew back into the bookshelf at the end of the hallway and crashed into it. He then fell to the floor and was knocked out. The loud noise of Drandon crashing back into the bookshelf sounded through the whole house. Jamie was the first to say something. "Is everything all right?" Jamie yelled upstairs as she climbed the stairs to see what had happened. When she got to the top of the stairs, she noticed Pete on the floor, and when she turned the corner, she saw Drandon on the floor, not moving, and noticed the bookshelf was shattered.

"What happened up here?" Jamie screamed as she ran over to where Drandon lay on the ground.

"He was hitting me and wouldn't leave me alone," Pete told his mother.

"I don't care! Do you know what you have done?" Jamie screamed at Pete.

"Yes, he was hurting me, and he was coming at me again, and all of a sudden he flew back into the shelf. I didn't mean to do anything like this. Even though he deserved it!" Pete yelled back at his mother.

Jamie said it was his entire fault. Everything was always his fault; no one ever took his side.

"I don't care. You could have killed him. His head is bleeding. Go call your grandfather. He needs to get over here and heal Drandon," Jamie ordered Pete.

At that moment Mark came up the stairs to investigate what had happened. When he saw his son on the ground with the bookshelf shattered behind him, he ran over to Pete and threw him against the wall.

"What did you do? You hurt my son!" Mark screamed at Pete, not even sure it was his fault but deciding it was.

"Get your hands off my son!" Jamie said in an angry voice that Pete had never heard before.

Mark dropped Pete and stepped back from him. Then he went over to Drandon. Mark picked him up and carried him out to the car. On his way out, he said, "I'm taking him to the hospital, and when I return I don't want to see that little brat the rest of the night."

Jamie turned to Pete now and said, "I'm sorry for all the yelling. I know you didn't mean to do anything to hurt him that bad. You're still learning about your powers and how to use them. This must be one you can't control yet. Don't worry about Mark finding out. We will tell him that you just pushed him back, and he tripped and landed on the shelf."

Pete couldn't believe what his mom was saying to him. She sounded like a totally different person than she was a few moments ago. She actually was taking his side for once since Drandon and Mark moved in.

"It's all right. Everything is going fine. I think I'll gain more control when I go to Goodrick's," Pete said to his mother in a polite tone.

"I think it would be the best if you go to the school now. It looks like you truly are a mutant sorcerer and need to practice with your power so you don't kill someone," Jamie said to Pete as she watched his face brighten.

Pete couldn't wait to go there. He had been waiting for six months already, and now he didn't have to wait any more.

"I'm going to call one of the assistants at the school to come and pick you up. He should arrive in a couple of hours, so go and pack up," Jamie told Pete.

Chapter Twelve

Pete went down into the basement to his room and started to pack. He would stay at the school until the summer. When he was packing pictures of his mom and dad, he saw a book that he had been planning to get down from the top of the shelf for a while now. After he packed the pictures, he got the book down. The book had no title, but there were symbols that looked like a different language and a picture of the sun and the moon on the cover. There was a picture of the necklace with the green eye on the front as well. Pete opened the cover and scrolled through the pages only to find more and more of the same kind of symbols that were on the cover. He found different pages that had pictures of dragons and different people that he assumed to be wizards. As he turned the pages, he found more pictures that were of the world and of people who had wings. He assumed the people to be angels and demons since some were black.

He decided to take the book with him. After he carefully packed the book, he got the rest of the things he needed and took his suitcase upstairs to wait for the person who would take him to Goodrick's School of Mutant and Wizard Sorcery. He was so excited about going and couldn't believe his mom was letting him go this early. She was always so worried about him. Pete knew she just cared about him.

After he got all of his stuff upstairs, his mother handed him a ham sandwich. He sat down and waited while he ate. After about five minutes, the doorbell rang. Jamie got up from the couch and went over to the door and opened it. A tall man with dark hair stood in the doorway and right away greeted Jamie.

"Hello, Jamie, how are you?" the man said while walking into the house.

"Oh, I was hoping it would be you. I'm fine. You?" Jamie asked him in return.

"As good as ever," the man proclaimed.

Jamie walked him over to where Pete was sitting to introduce him. "Pete, this is Miguel Johnson. He works at the school you're going to. He was an old friend of your father's."

"How are you, Pete? You look so much like your father," Miguel told Pete.

"I'm fine, thanks," Pete replied.

"Well then, I guess it's time to leave. The sub leaves at exactly eight oh seven. So we don't have much time to waste," Miguel told Pete as Pete went over to grab his things.

"How far do we have to go? I won't have to carry all my stuff all the way to the train station, will I?" Pete asked as he picked up his suitcase.

"No. Here, let me help you a bit," Miguel said. He pulled out from inside his pocket a little wooden stick that had what looked like leaf buds around the entire length of it.

This was the first time Pete had ever seen a wand. His mom didn't want him around them until the time he would go to school. Miguel took his wand and gave it a wave toward Pete's bags. The leaf buds glowed white as the bags disappeared with a small pop.

"Thanks," Pete said to Miguel.

"Now you won't have to carry them all the way," Miguel told Pete. "It's going to be quite the ride this year," Miguel said excitedly.

Pete went over to his mom and gave her a hug and kiss and said good-bye. Miguel and Pete started out of the house when they heard Jamie yell, "Wait!" Jamie came over into the doorway and handed Pete a small, rectangular-shaped box. "This used to be your father's. It is very important you don't open it until you get to school," Jamie told Pete while a tear rolled down from her eye.

"All right, see you in a few months!" Pete yelled back to her as Miguel and he walked down the sidewalk.

"All right, grab onto my arm tightly. We can't just walk there. We have to enter in a different way," Miguel ordered Pete.

Pete listened to him. As soon as Pete grasped onto Miguel's arm, the whole world surrounding him swirled just like what had happened when he touched his necklace. He and Miguel were spinning around a huge tunnel that appeared to be covered in blue fire. It seemed as if they were going really fast, as if they were in a vortex. The magical community called it a *teleportation vortex*. As they spun, Pete noticed that a large building was coming into view, and they appeared inside.

CHAPTER THIRTEEN

There was a huge black submarine that had hundreds of people surrounding it. Through the many windows that lined the sides of the submarine, faces of other kids that were going to Goodrick's could be seen peering out at the remaining people waiting to board the sub. The lines trailed a ways before Pete could get on, though.

The submarine had neon cords that shined blue running down the sides and around the windows along with large squares that looked like huge microchips lining the top and underside of the cybercon sub. These defined features allowed for a more concise magnetic field to be created for the submarine to be able to transport larger quantities at greater speeds to a certain location, just like how Miguel transported Pete, but with a greater effect.

"All right, it's time for me to go. I'll see you at school later tonight," Miguel said while walking away.

Pete went over to the cybercon sub and waited in line until he was able to get aboard. As he was walking down the train aisle to find a seat, he noticed a girl with dark-blonde hair was sitting by herself. He went over to where she was and sat down next to her. The girl turned and faced him and smiled. Her teeth were sparkling white, and they shined even though the light in the room was dim. Her hair was wavy and looked very clean and fresh. She looked like royalty. Her dress was pearl white, not a stain on it. She was one of the prettiest girls Pete had ever seen.

Pete didn't hear what she said the first time she said it, but the second time she caught his attention. "What's your name?"

"My name is Pete, Pete Winfield." And then he asked her, "Have you ever been to Goodrick's before?"

"Yeah, this will be my third year. It's a really fun school. What ability do you have?" the girl asked Pete while smiling.

"I'm a mutant and a wizard. I have the mutant gene of immortality, and I'm a wizard too. I got the mutant gene from my mother and the wizard gift from my father," Pete told the girl. "What's your name?" Pete asked, remembering he hadn't asked her yet.

"I'm Lucy," she said back to him.

"So what's this school like?" Pete asked.

"Just like any other school, I suppose. Except that we get to do so much more due to our gifts that all of us have. Have you ever been to a mortal school?"

"That's where I have been until now. I couldn't stand it there. They have no perception about life. They take things for granted so much. They don't look at what nature really has to offer."

"Oh I know. I only went there for two years, thank goodness. We left there after my father died."

"Oh, I'm sorry. My father died too, but I never got to meet him. You've heard of him, haven't you, George Winfield?"

"The name isn't ringing a bell, but who knows? Maybe I have." She got a weird look on her face.

"So a submarine. Quite a catchy ride huh?" Pete asked.

"Yeah, she's served the Xertan colony ever since my mother was in school. Which is a long time," she chuckled.

"It must take a long time to get there."

"Nope, not long at all. You'll see."

After she said that, they felt the submarine start to move and heard it sound its horn. While it started to move out slowly, a lady's voice came through the speakers that were on top of the ceiling in the sub.

"Everyone, take your seats. You only have thirty seconds before we take off completely. So if you don't want to get badly injured, then I suggest you sit down with your hands in your lap."

All the kids hurried into their seats after the lady said that. And after every seat in the entire sub was taken, metal safety belts came up through the sides of the seats and around the kid's shoulders. The safety belts encaged them like a roller coaster bar. No one could hardly move an inch with the belts encaged around them.

The submarine started to move faster as it moved into a dark tunnel. It was a good thing they had safety belts on because as soon as they were completely in the tunnel, the sub began to free fall with its nose first. The sub had to have been going three hundred miles an hour. As it picked up speed, the nose of the sub burst into blue flames. The flames swirled around the large microchips on top of the sub and below with more energy being added to them from the neon blue veins that straddled the frame of the cybercon sub. The flames grew larger until finally the sub stretched and entered a large vortex that had formed in the water.

The sub traced across the open waters of the Great Ocean going at an unimaginable speed. Pete sat back in his seat, unable to move or blink. He had no idea what was going on. All of a sudden the train stopped abruptly and crept its way up to the surface. The gigantic cybercon sub floated toward a dock that lined the edge of a dark hill that rolled up to the colony of Xerta and the gates that went into the school.

Also when they stopped, the safety belts detached and went back into the seats as if they were never there. Immediately everyone got up from their seats. Some were puzzled by what just happened, Pete being one of them, since it was their first time on the sub. Pete noticed the box that his mom had given him had been thrown away from where he was and landed under the seat across from him. He quickly retrieved it.

The doors to the sub finally opened up, and kids poured out of them, exiting the docking platform. Pete followed Lucy as she followed the rest of the crowd. There were huge doors that led them out of the station onto a huge sidewalk that led up to the largest building Pete had ever seen. Even though it was nighttime, the entire building was lit up from the window light shining out onto the grounds surrounding the school. From what Pete could tell, the school buildings were made of a mixture of the buildings of a castle and a modern-day school. The building was the largest structure he had ever seen. The towers from the castle part were thousands of feet up, and the other structures that looked like a regular school were larger than he expected as he walked closer. In the foreground Pete could see lights shining from the colony up into the clouds above.

In the group of kids Pete was walking with, there had to be several hundred. When they reached the doors—that was the entrance to the school—the doors were hung on a huge archway. The man who was leading the crowd of kids to the school knocked on the door with some kind of secret knock, and the doors began to open.

When the doors opened, they let out light, shining across the grounds all around the school. Pete looked back to where the light shined and saw in the distance some kind of body of water. When he turned back around, the man that was leading the group had gone inside the school as the crowd of several hundred kids began to follow him.

When Pete and Lucy reached the huge archway doors and entered the building, Pete could not believe what he was seeing. The ceiling of the entrance way was a huge cathedral ceiling that had pictures lining the walls all the way up to the top where a huge crystal light structure lit up the entire room. The crowd of kids followed the man in front into a long hall that had tables in the middle and on the far end were two levels of tables, one on the ground level among the rest and the other up top on what was the second story of that end.

Pete's first impression of the room was that it must be the dining hall. There were at least a thousand chairs for people to sit down in along the tables. More than half of the seats were taken from other kids, and the rest of the seats were taken as the group of kids Pete was with sat down. Pete and Lucy sat down next to each other. Pete sat there, looking up at the huge dining hall, amazed at how large it was. It too had a cathedral ceiling but not as large as the entrance hall. On the side walls of the dining hall were tall, skinny windows that appeared every ten feet. On the left side of where the two long tables sat in the front of the hall there was a large window.

As Pete was admiring the large structure, the teachers of the school had lined the tables in front of the hall and sat down in their chairs. There was one large, golden chair lined with emeralds in front of which an average-sized man with a brown goatee and hair stood. He had sapphire-colored eyes and wore glasses that sat at the tip of his nose.

The man began to talk loud enough so his voice echoed through the entire hall. "Welcome. Today is the first day of the second semester here at Goodrick's school. I welcome all of you back after the long break, and I welcome the new students here today who will start here for the first time. We have added some new buildings onto the school, which will hold new classrooms and living areas for some of you for the next few months. There are also some new restrictions this semester: the most important one you must follow is do not enter the east wing of the school if you don't want to be badly injured or even killed. We have some new experiments we're trying out in there, and that is all I can tell you. Now let's eat," the man finished as he sat down.

When the man finished, there were short little women that came out of these big doors at the north end of the dinner hall with huge pots of food balanced on their heads. The women went down between the tables and lined the tables with the food. All the kids began to eat as the food came to them. When the food reached Pete, it was the best-smelling food he had ever smelled. It was also the best tasting. There was turkey, potatoes, ham, fruit, chocolate-covered peanuts, cake, ice cream, and soup. Pete tried a little of everything.

After the feast was over, Pete asked Lucy, "What is the name of that guy up there sitting in the golden chair?"

Lucy swallowed the food she had in her mouth and replied, "That's Professor Goodrick. He teaches advanced students about curses and jinxes. I have been in his class since last year. I almost made it in the first year, but I wasn't powerful enough. He knows his stuff. Have you ever read the book *The Mysteries We Never Knew Existed* by Matthew Goodrick?"

"No, I really don't read. I know a lot about the magical world, just not much through books. My mom sent me here to learn more so that I can control my powers, though," Pete told Lucy.

As they finished eating, the little women came around the table again and picked up the leftovers and the dirty dishes. Up at the teacher's table in the front of the hall, two of the teachers got up with a stack of papers and set them down onto the tables.

The hall went quiet as one of the teachers echoed across the hall, "It's time to get your schedules and your living space. Clear all things off your table so the schedule sheets can find where you are."

The woman scanned the room to make sure no one's hands were on the table. Then she took out her wand and tapped the stack of papers in front of her. The papers began to fly off the stack and to their owners. When Pete's reached him, the paper had his name on it with a list of classes under it.

Pete Arthur Winfield

> Period 1: Creatures among the Mist—
> Teacher: Professor Hark

> Period 2: Mutant Sorcery—
> Teacher: Professor Sowles

> Period 3: Wizard Sorcery—
> Teacher: Professor Johnson

> Period 4: The Dark Ages—
> Teacher: Professor Star

> Living Area: NW1292—
> Second Floor

Pete sat there looking at his schedule, wondering what the classes would be like. He turned to Lucy and asked her, "Where are all these places? Isn't there a map or something I can get to find all my classes?"

"Yeah, after dinner, come with me to the main office where the school sells them. You'll like it a lot. It shows you where everything is," Lucy answered him.

After dinner Lucy took Pete to a room just past the main office just outside the dinner hall, down a hallway off the entrance hall. When they arrived Pete walked into the room, wondering what the heck in there could possibly take him to all of his classes. All that was in there was small-sized statue figures of different animals. Pete was still carrying around the box his mom gave him and decided to open it. He took the top off, only to find a silver-and-green crystal-material wand that was in no way the same kind that Miguel had.

"Wow, I got my own wand," Pete said happily. He picked it up and saw that there was a note inside of the box too. The note read:

> Dear Pete,
>   This wand used to be your father's. It is one of the greatest wands ever made throughout history. I have saved it since your father passed away. I'm sure he would want you to have it. Hope you have lots of fun at school.
>
> Love, Mom
> P.S. Write back soon.

After Pete read the letter, his whole body felt weak, and he collapsed to the floor. When he hit the floor, a surge of strength went through his whole body. He was in the green haze again, but this time all he could hear was "Pete, Pete, are you all right?"

Chapter Fourteen

When Pete came back to the normal world, Lucy was sitting over him, shaking him, trying to wake him back up. When he opened his eyes, they flashed green, but Lucy didn't notice. Pete felt all of his strength come back to him as he stood up.

"Is something wrong?" Lucy asked.

"No, I'm all right. Just felt a little faint, that's all," Pete replied. "Everything is all right. It's normal," Pete told Lucy, trying to get the worried look off her face.

Lucy got Pete to stand up and led him into the large room that was behind where the main office was in the Entrance Hall. Pete's attention was turned from him collapsing to the small creature statues.

"What are they?" Pete asked.

"They're Mapbuddies, at least that's what I call them. They are actually Info-pets. They're built from an informative jinx. Watch this," Lucy said while walking up to a shelf that had little horse statues on it.

She reached out her hand, and as soon as the tip of her finger touched the rocky surface of the horse, life spread from where the connection was made. Brown and white hair soon covered the now beautiful model-sized horse.

"I lost mine last semester after he fell out of my bag, still as a statue, and it went down four flights of stairs, shattering on impact." Lucy said while almost crying.

"Oh, what's wrong?"

"When you get these, you get attached to them quite quickly. They help you find anything throughout this place. My last one saved my life after I almost fell down off a cliff when it was pitch black out. For how little they are, they sure do have some strength."

"I'm sorry. That's too bad. What one do you think I should get?" Pete gasped with excitement. He never had gotten his own pet before, especially one that was a statue part of the time. He went looking down the rest of the shelf for what would be his info-pet.

"Gelden. That is what I will call you," Lucy spoke to her new info-pet.

The horse replied in a deep man's voice, "Gelden I am. How may I be of service to you, madam?"

"I don't need you quite yet. You can go back to sleep. I was just showing my friend here how you guys work."

"No problem. When you do need me, just give me a rub." Gelden snorted and froze back into his statue formation.

"Hey, I think I found which one I want!" Pete yelled from down on the other end of the shelf.

Lucy walked down there and saw that Pete was looking at a dragon. "Oh look, it's the only one left," Lucy pointed out to Pete.

"Oh, you're right. It sure is. That's why I must get it," Pete said while reaching out to touch the rock-scales of the dragon.

When his finger met the rock-scale of the dragon, Pete could feel the sharpness of it. The armored skin thickened at his touch. He felt an instant emotional connection. He felt attached so quickly.

"Why do I feel him?" Pete sensed the dragon's thoughts.

"Dragons, I believe, tend to have greater attachments to their owners and people. They are thought to do that because of their great abilities in defense. One must really care to sacrifice their life for one they defend."

"The jinx works to that extent, huh?"

"Yeah, that's why they recommend every student here to get one. I've never seen a dragon here before. They must be rare or something. Or maybe you just got lucky," she said with a smirk on her face.

"She's right, Pete. Quite a bright one you are, little missy," the dragon spoke in a Prore' accent. Prore' people came from the eastern lands on the other side of the Great Ocean.

"Sid shall be your name," Pete said while smiling.

"Come on. We need to go pay."

"You can go to sleep," Pete said to Sid.

The dragon got into position and instantly turned to stone. Pete and Lucy walked up to the counter with their two new info-pets and called for the cashier. She made her way over quite slowly, and Pete noticed she had a limp. The woman was elderly and had silver hair. Her face was stained with wrinkles, and she could barely speak.

"Hello, children. You got two info-pets?"

"Yes, ma'am. How much are they?" Pete asked.

"It'll be seven coins for the horse and fourteen for the dragon."

They both paid and went on their way out of the store.

"Get out your dragon and rub down his spine. Then say, 'awaken,'" Lucy ordered.

Pete did what she said, and as he did, Sid came back to life.

Sid crawled up onto Pete's shoulder and perched himself by sitting down like a dog.

"All right, where we off to, mate?" Sid asked.

"Living space northwest 1292," Pete responded.

"All righty, go down this hall and take the flight of stairs. When you get on the second floor, you need to go straight off the stairs and then take a right," Sid spoke very clearly and informatively.

"Okay, I'll get on that then."

Lucy followed Pete and Sid. She left Gelden in her purse that she carried. They got to the straight part of the second floor and turned right. They waited next for Sid to give them more directions.

"You know I think I had us go the wrong way. Turn around," Sid ordered. Pete started to turn around. "Oh I'm only jokin,'" Sid started to laugh while spitting out a little fire. "Walk down the rest of the hall and take a left, and then go down until you find the Fountain of Glory."

When they reached the fountain, they were in a giant, circular room that had five hallways meeting in one. The opening of the ceiling reached up four stories.

"The hallway you seek is straight ahead, northwest wing. Your room is fourteen doors down on the right."

In the center of the room was the fountain that was named on a plaque in the center of the tank, which held the Fountain of Glory.

Pete and Lucy walked straight over to the northwest hallway and followed the hallway down and found the fourteenth door on the right side, labeled 1292. Pete started to turn the doorknob to his living space, but when he touched the knob, the paint on the door began to ripple and shape into the form of a mouth.

After it emerged, the mouth began to speak, "I am the security system of the school. This seems weird, but I have to do it. What is your name?" The mouth asked after it explained why it just emerged out of a wall.

"P-Pete," Pete said, looking at the mouth, amazed.

"How old are you?" it asked again.

"Fifteen," Pete answered it.

Lucy was standing back from Pete, smiling because on her first day here the same thing happened to her.

"Why are you here?" the mouth asked politely.

"I—I'm here to learn how to control my powers," Pete answered it, kind of mumbling.

"You have passed the test. Now put your hand on my tongue, that way each time you twist the handle, it will automatically unlock for you so that you can get in here from now on," the mouth told Pete.

The mouth stuck out a long tongue and Pete put his hand on it. *How disgusting*. The mouth was even warm.

The mouth immersed itself back into the paint of the doorway and vanished. When Pete reached for the doorknob, the door opened by itself. Pete stepped through his doorway to find a medium-sized room with a small bunk on one side and all of his clothes and stuff spread across it. On the other side, there was a dresser where he could put his clothes. There was also a small window in the back of the room that looked over the school grounds.

Lucy had left Pete in his room to get all of his stuff in order. She went down to her new room, and the same mouth appeared out of the paint of the door and began to ask her questions. After she put her hand on the tongue of the mouth, the door to her room opened to reveal all of her clothes and stuff that she had in her old room. She too had a small window looking out onto the school grounds.

As Pete and Lucy were going through all their stuff, a voice began to speak through loudspeakers that were in each corner of the rooms, "Attention, all students! Classes will start at eight sharp tomorrow morning. Please bring the bags that are located on your desks in the corner of your living spaces. These hold all of the supplies for your classes. I advise you to purchase a school info-pet if you are new to our school so you are not late to class. Being late is not accepted past the first day. Also tomorrow morning is our first breakfast together since coming back from break. Breakfast will be at seven sharp tomorrow morning, one hour before classes start. I hope everyone found their living space and all of you have a good night," the man finished. Pete had heard that voice before. He thought for a moment and finally realized that it was Miguel.

Sid jumped down off from Pete's shoulder and flew over atop of his desk in the corner. "Goodnight, Sir Pete. I shall see you in the morning," Sid said while positioning again and then going back to his hardened state.

Pete noticed that Lucy had left, so he closed his door. He looked at his watch and saw that it was almost eleven. He got his nightclothes on and went over to lie down on his bunk. As soon as he gave up all his strength to his sleep, the green-eyed necklace began to glow. But this time Pete wasn't just in a green haze; his whole body was engulfed in green flames, and he began to travel through a long tunnel that never seemed to end. But when it did, the only thing that came into sight was nothing but darkness.

Chapter Fifteen

Pete was on the floor of what seemed to be a large room. As he lay there, he noticed that the room had windows along the sides of it. A bright light caught his attention and an echo from someone's voice said, "Lighten factula." The light exploded in the center of the rooms' ceiling, engulfing the large room with light. A noticeable figure emerged from the end of the room and came walking over to Pete. As the figure came into better view, he recognized it was his father. George had his wand out, ready to attack anything that moved.

Pete started to run toward his father to greet him. The place Pete was in now wasn't like the green haze he had been in when his father told him about the powers the necklace held. This place seemed real. As Pete got closer to his father, he stopped to greet him, but his father kept walking. George was walking right toward Pete, and Pete didn't move. He walked straight through Pete as if he was a ghost.

Pete turned around to see where George was going. And now he realized why George had his wand raised. There was a huge door at the end George was walking toward. George stopped, and the door exploded into a million pieces, and the explosion shot the pieces across the room, hitting George.

In the doorway appeared a tall man with a long, black cloak on. He too had a wand raised, ready to fight. Pete was blind to who the man standing in the doorway was. Pete looked closer at the other dueler and noticed that around his neck was a necklace with an eye in the center of it. But that necklace wasn't green; it was red. Pete also looked at his dad's neck and saw the same necklace that Pete was wearing.

The mysterious man and George looked at each other for a moment, and then the man raised his wand and whipped it at George. A bolt of red light shot out of the tip of the wand and hit George. George blocked with a shield that magically surrounded him. The mysterious man's necklace began to glow as he sent more bolts of light at George. His eyes began to glow red. George's shield didn't let any of the man's curses through. The shield was too powerful.

They were fighting for a while until the other wizard whipped his wand up into the air toward the ceiling. There was a force that came from his wand that hit the ceiling, causing it to rip apart. Chunks of rock fell from the ceiling and tumbled down toward George. George was too fast for the rocks and sent shocks of green light at them, causing them to explode. Now the man became angry. He slashed his wand and arms around toward the windows that lined the room, shattering them into tiny little pieces of glass.

The red-eyed man clapped his hands together, making the little pieces of glass fly toward George. The shield around George became like a wall and stopped all the pieces in mid air. George's eyes began to glow green as the necklace illuminated. The man backed away from George, visibly in shock.

George's body was engulfed in green flames as a force field exploded around his body, crashing into his shield and turning the glass into dust. The explosion caused the mystery man to fly back and hit the floor. When he fell, his wand fell out of his hand. The whole room was engulfed in a green force field as George walked to where the man lay on the ground. He could barely sit up because of the strength of the force field emanating from George.

When George reached the man he raised his wand at him and said, "I take all the power vested in me by the seven courts and banish you. You shall not take another step with the power of the seven courts around you."

After George said that, a bolt of golden light shot out of the tip of his wand and hit the man's red-eyed necklace, causing the red stone embedded in the necklace to crack down the middle. The chain around the man's neck broke and floated up to George. George grabbed the red-eyed necklace. The force field that was around George lifted as the green-eyed necklace stopped glowing along with George's eyes. The man lay on the ground, trembling as his body caught fire. He began to scream from the pain of his body being engulfed in flames. Eventually the flames caused his body to vanish. The man was nowhere to be found.

Pete stood in the background in the shadows of the room, cautious of what might happen if he went out there. He heard every word and saw everything that had happened between his dad and the other wizard. He stood there watching his dad walk from the back of the room where he came from and vanish into the shadows. Pete saw a flash of green light, and his dad was gone.

The room started to twist around and turn into a green haze as Pete's body was engulfed in green flames, and he went through the same tunnel he came there in and returned to his bed back at school.

The necklace that was around his neck was glowing just like it had when Pete's father wore it around his neck during that battle Pete just witnessed. He had no idea what that was all about, but the one thing that shocked him the most was he never knew his dad was that powerful. Pete also got to see the power of the green necklace at its weakest. As Pete lay on his bed, he heard something move over in the corner of his room and discovered that the outline of Miguel Johnson was standing there.

CHAPTER SIXTEEN

"What are you doing in here?" Pete said. He was startled to see Miguel in his room.

"Oh, I'm sorry to intrude, but I sensed that something had gone on and that you weren't in the school," Miguel said back.

"How did you know I wasn't here?" Pete asked.

"I was tracking you on my map that tells me where everyone is. It's part of the new security system," Miguel explained to Pete. "I know about the necklace, Pete. I saw you wearing it when I first came to your house. When we got here to school, I kept an eye on you to make sure nothing bad happened to you," Miguel told Pete.

"How do you know about it?" asked Pete.

"Remember, I used to be your father's friend. He too had the necklace. But since he died, it came to you.

There's a lot you need to know," Miguel said while sitting down next to Pete. "I take it you have brought the book?" Miguel questioned.

"Yeah, I got it," Pete answered after realizing what book Miguel was talking about.

Pete went over to his suitcase and found the book. He got it out and brought it over to his bed. Miguel brought his wand out from under his cloak and pointed it at the light that was in the corner, causing it to brighten. Miguel grabbed the book from Pete.

"This is indeed the true book. The original writing. Your father showed me this before, but he couldn't read any of it except one tiny sentence." Miguel flipped the book over and pointed to a small sentence at the bottom. Now Miguel read it aloud: "The one who reads the book is the chosen one—*the Emerald Prince*. The one who cannot can only pass it on."

"What does that mean?" Pete asked with a confused look on his face.

"It means if you cannot read the inside of the book using the power of the necklace, then you are not the Emerald Prince, but if you can, then you will read the book to conquer all the powers the necklace holds inside of it," Miguel finished while handing the book to Pete.

"But what does 'the Emerald Prince' mean?" asked Pete.

"That is what I shall explain to you after you find out if you can read the book," Miguel told Pete.

"Take out your wand and touch the tip of it to the center of the eye of the necklace on the front. The necklace you wear around your neck will react to the connection, and if you are the Emerald Prince, then you will be able to read the book," Miguel explained.

Pete got his wand out and touched the tip of it to the center of the necklace on the front of the book. As soon as they touched together, they created a spark. The book began to illuminate as the pages inside the book began to glow. Pete opened the book and saw that the symbols that were once there were turning into words that Pete could actually read.

"Can you read them?" Miguel asked anxiously.

"Yes, yes I can. Now what?" Pete said nervously. At the sound of "the Emerald Prince," he realized he had no idea what he was in store for.

"This means that the element embedded in the necklace you wear has finally found its true owner," Miguel said. "Pete, there are a lot of things you need to know and not a lot of time to learn them. So listen to me very carefully," Miguel said, waiting for Pete to give him all of his attention. "This necklace you wear around your neck is the most powerful magical thing on this planet. What I am about to tell you might come to you as a joke, but it is not. I am going to tell you all I know. Do not ask questions please," Miguel said, now with full attention from Pete.

"The necklace you wear around your neck was sent here from the almighty one himself. It is one of his many plans to fight the war between good and evil. The almighty one has many plans for the planet he has created. The most-known plan was when he sent a messenger to our world whose name is unknown. This plan brought wizardry to the world. Only a select few were chosen to be a witch or wizard. The almighty one's messenger only reached some of the people in the world, not all of them. But some of this plan failed, and the almighty one knew it would. Some of the newly made witches and wizards turned over to the evil side, leaving the good wizard population smaller.

"So he came up with another plan. He would change the way his plan would work out for revolution. He would change it at one split second of time on the world he built. This is where your necklace comes into play. The almighty one sent an element straight from the heavens that hit the world, going straight to the world's core. All I know is at that split second, thousands died, thousands were diseased, and thousands developed a mutation. This is when mutants came to our world. That's all I know, but tomorrow after you're done for the day, we're going to go to see an old friend of my father," Miguel finished.

"Can I ask a question?" Pete asked.

"Nope. Answers will come to those questions tomorrow. Now go to sleep and take all that information in. You will need to know the full story," Miguel said then paused. "I expect your life here will soon be very active and full of excitement," Miguel said as he left. "The majority from here on out will not even include school."

Pete lay back down, thinking about what Miguel had told him. He still had the book in his hand but decided not to read it. He set the book down under his bed and turned the light off. Pete went back over to his bed and lay down once again to fall asleep.

CHAPTER SEVENTEEN

When Pete awoke, he soon found out from looking at his watch that it was six thirty. Breakfast was in half an hour. Pete got up and got dressed. He grabbed his bag that had all his supplies in it and his wand and set out to eat. He met up with Lucy in the room where all the hallways came together on the second floor and walked with her to the dining hall. When they got there, the tables were just starting to fill with people. Lucy and Pete found a spot where they wanted to eat and sat down. Soon after they got there, the rest of the school piled into the hall and sat to wait for the short ladies to bring them food. The doors opened as the ladies came out with pots on their heads, packed with food.

There were pancakes, French toast, sausage, bacon, gravy, biscuits, milk, and juice. Pete just realized how hungry he had gotten, but really it was just his nerves. He ate until he was full and got up and said good-bye to Lucy and went off to his first class.

Pete took out his school map and schedule to look at where his first class was. His first period was Creatures among the Mist taught by Professor Hark. He got Sid out and told him to guide the way to the class. Sid immediately rambled on about the directions. Pete listened and followed them.

He followed the directions until he reached a dark hallway that led to a tall door at the end. He was nervous at first but made his way to the end and saw engraved in gold, Creatures among the Mist, Professor Hark. Pete opened the door only to find a room filled with cages along the walls with strange animals in them that Pete had never seen. Pete walked in, seeing a few kids in there already, and turned the corner to find the whole room. The half that Pete saw first was the smaller half lined with cages. The other half of the room was triple the size with a taller ceiling. In the corner of the larger room, there was an enclosed cage with see-through glass that, from what Pete could see, held a small dragon.

Pete, growing excited already about the class, went to the back row of seats closest to the door and sat down. He sat there for about five minutes until a lot more kids came into the room, also admiring the creatures that lined the walls. All the kids took their seats. A minute later, Pete heard the sound of a bell echo into the room. He assumed that it must be the start of class.

After the bell rang, a small creature jumped up onto the desk in front of the room. The creature looked like a small cheetah crossed with a dog. The creature screeched and jumped off the desk toward the kids in the front row and transformed into a short man with the same-colored hair the cheetah dog had. Everyone in the front row jumped back, and the girls screamed.

"Hello, what a pleasure it is to have you in my class," the man said. He looked at the kids' scared faces in the front row and throughout the room. "Now I know that might have scared you, but if you want to be in my class, you have to have a little more bravery than that," the man said while eyeing the girls in the front row.

"My name is Professor Hark, and I will be your teacher for this class, Creatures among the Mist," Hark said while walking around his desk. "In this class we will learn about animal genetics and how we can crossbreed them in our society, and how we can do it in the wild as well," Hark scanned the room while talking. "Now, today, since it is the first day of classes, we will play games all hour," he said, watching everyone's face get excited. "Of course, I'm only joking, partially. The games will be your first test on what you know about animals and their characteristics," Hark proclaimed while watching the faces of all the excited kids go back to their original state.

Hark walked over to a shelf where there were cages that had different animals in them. He grabbed two of the cages and set them down in front of a girl in the front row. The girl became really scared and backed her chair away from the table as far as she could until she hit the table behind her.

"I want everyone to take out the blue notebook labeled Creatures among the Mist, and take out a pen or pencil as well," Hark ordered. All the kids grabbed the notebook labeled Creatures among the Mist out of their supply bags and put them in front of themselves along with a pen or pencil. "Who can tell me what the animal on the right is crossbred with?" Hark asked.

Pete looked at the animal closely to see the characteristics of it. To him it looked like a fox. But its fur resembled a raccoon. Pete raised his hand. "The animal looks like a fox crossbred with a raccoon."

The animal turned and had the same hind legs and tail as a raccoon as well. "Correct," Hark said, with some hope in his look that someone knew something about animals. "Yes, this animal here is called a racox," Hark explained. "This racox's mother was a raccoon, and its father was a fox. This animal is very rare in the wild. It is usually only created in labs, but there are some cases in which they have been created in the wild. Thank you..." Hark said, pausing, awaiting for Pete to tell him his name.

"Pete."

"Thank you, Pete," Hark finished.

"Now, who can tell what this animal is on my left?" Hark questioned, scanning the room for other guessers. Pete looked at this one and could only think that it was a cross between a cat, squirrel, and a rat. The animal had the face of a squirrel but the ears and the body of a cat, and it had the tail of a rat. Pete didn't answer, but another kid sitting in the middle of the room raised his hand.

"Yes, what do think it is?" Hark asked the kid.

"Is it a squirrel and a rat?" the kid questioned for an answer.

"Ah, not quite. You're right, but it also has feline in it. This is a squirrel, rat, and a cat. The mother was a cat, but the father was a cross between a squirrel and a rat. The father is called a squat, and this animal is called a feline squat," Hark finished.

Professor Hark put the cages back onto the shelf where they were before and started around the room to tell the class about other animals. The class soon ended after Hark handed out the textbooks they would be using. Pete got one that must have been a hundred years old, but none of the other ones were any better.

Chapter Eighteen

Pete headed off to his next class, which was Mutant Sorcery taught by Professor Sowles. As he looked in his bag for Sid to get directions, Lucy came up behind him to walk with him until she reached her class.

"How was your first class?" Lucy asked Pete.

"It was fun. We played a game all hour," Pete responded, smiling.

"What class was it again?" Lucy questioned.

"Creatures among the Mist," Pete answered.

"Oh, yeah, I remember that class. We played a game on my first day too. We played the guessing game," Lucy told Pete.

"We played the same thing," Pete told her.

"Well, I gotta go. I guess I'll see you at lunch," Lucy said as she turned the corner and left. Pete said good-bye.

Pete had to go to the huge staircase in the center of the castle. When he reached it, there was a small door hidden behind one of the staircases that led to his next class. When he got to the door, he opened it to find a small stairway going down. He followed it until he reached another door, which was labeled Mutant Sorcery.

Pete opened the door to find a huge room with cathedral ceiling just like the dining hall. He walked in to find a woman in the front of the room sitting at a desk—he assumed that she was Professor Sowles—along with kids sitting in chairs along tables that were in front of her.

He walked down to find a seat. As he walked by other kids, he noticed that some of them had something wrong with them. One kid had dark-black eyes with horns sticking out of his head, and this girl had long, black hair with white stripes, and her fingernails were black. It was a long time since he had ever seen anyone with these kinds of features. The last time he saw someone with a mutant feature was back when he was in preschool.

Pete finally found a seat in the third row. After he sat down, about ten other kids came in and sat down as well. When the last person sat down, the teacher in front got up and began to speak. "Good morning, class. And welcome to Mutant Sorcery. Now, there is not a lot that we have to do today, but I would like to have everyone stand up and introduce themselves and tell the class what kind of gift they have. I will go first," the teacher said while taking a deep breath.

"My name is Professor Sowles. I teach young children and young adults like yourselves how to control and progress their mutant powers. My gift as a mutant is that I am able to use powers that someone else possesses. I can copy that power and use it at my own will. Depending how long I am around that particular person is the amount of time I can mimic their power. I have been working here for the past four years and have worked in this industry for ten," Sowles finished. "All right, we'll start with you back there," Sowles said while pointing to the girl Pete had walked by with the black hair and nails.

The girl stood up and began to speak nervously, "Hi, my name is Kelly. When I was born there was evidence of me having a mutant gift already. Mine is that I'm really strong. I can lift almost anything. This is my second year here at this school," Kelly said as she sat back down.

All the kids had gone except for Pete. Professor Sowles called on him to stand up and tell the class about himself. "My name is Pete. I have the mutational gift of being immortal—I cannot die. I can get cut or hit, and the wound that occurs will heal itself quickly. So I guess regeneration comes along with it. This is my first year here at Goodrick's," Pete said while he too sat back down.

During the rest of the class, all of the kids were separated into two groups. Each group had to come up in front of the class and show the class what they could do. When Pete got up there with his group, he got a pencil out and cut the whole length of his arm open. Soon after he cut himself, the cut healed back to normal. The whole class was amazed. The rest of his group consisted of a telekinetic girl, a boy who could make things turn into ice, and another girl who could make fire.

The girl that had super strength picked up the teacher's desk to show the class what she could do. There was a boy who could breathe underwater and also a girl who could do the same thing, but she grew gills like a fish. There was also a girl who could imitate any living thing. She turned herself into the teacher. She didn't look entirely like the teacher but close enough that the whole class was impressed.

When class was over, Pete met up with Lucy in the entrance hall. When they arrived, Miguel was in the corner, looking for someone. When Miguel noticed Pete, Pete knew the person he was looking for was himself.

Miguel came over to where Pete was and began to speak. "Pete, we have to go right now. He's at home, and he only has a little while before he has to leave."

"Where do we have to go? I'm hungry. I don't want to leave," Pete said as he kept walking.

"The one who is to tell you who you really are," Miguel said while grabbing Pete's arm and looking him in the eyes.

"Oh," Pete said with a surprised expression.

"I got to go, Lucy. I'll see you later," Pete said while walking away with Miguel.

"Bye," said Lucy while turning, wondering why Pete had to go.

As Pete walked away alongside Miguel, his last thought after turning away from Lucy was that the school was too easy, just like public school had been. He felt he had larger things in store for him. He not only wouldn't have a normal life, but for the reason of not having a normal life, he could be the Emerald Prince.

Chapter Nineteen

Miguel took Pete down the corridor to the forbidden section that Goodrick told everyone to stay away from. They came up to a large archway with huge, wooden doors that filled it. At the bottom of the two doors, in the center, were two smaller doors. Miguel took out his wand and gave it a wave at the door and said something under his breath that Pete didn't hear. The doors swung open, and Pete followed Miguel through them. They entered a large room that was completely empty.

"I thought we had to stay out of here because there was something dangerous," Pete said to Miguel.

Miguel didn't say anything but went over to one of the sidewalls of the room to where the wall was pushed back into the shape of a rectangle. It was like a closet but with no doors.

"Come in here with me. And hold on tightly," Miguel ordered Pete. Pete grabbed a hold of Miguel's arm tightly. "All right, hang on," Miguel said.

Pete looked up at the top of the small closet-shaped spot in the wall and noticed there was a small pipe at the top.

"Miguel, what are we doing?" Pete asked.

"We're going to travel at the speed of light," Miguel responded.

As soon as he said that, a large drop of a cloudy look-ing substance came out from the pipe. It fell on top of Miguel's head. As soon as it touched Miguel, the sub-stance turned into a larger amount, causing a wave of the cloudy substance to engulf both Miguel and Pete.

The substance swirled around them until they van-ished. They were floating in what seemed to be a cloud at an enormous speed. They kept flying until a hole was formed in the side of what seemed to be a cloud, and they flew through it. A whole new world came into view as they came crashing down to the ground. There was a small cabin nearby, and they were standing on sand. Pete turned around and noticed that they were somewhere out in the middle of the ocean. Waves calmly splashed up along the sandy shore of the beach. The wind had a warm crisp smell to it like paradise. There was no other land in sight beside that upon which they stood.

When Pete turned back around, he noticed that Miguel was headed up to the cabin. When Pete reached him, Miguel was already knocking on the door. As the two of them stood there, the handle to the door turned, and the door opened to reveal a short, stout man with white hair and a short white beard.

"Miguel, I have been expecting you," the man said excitedly.

"I have been longing to see you as well," Miguel said.

"This is Pete, and, Pete, this is one of my father's old friends, Benjamin Walkman," Miguel said, introducing Pete and Ben to each other. Pete and Ben shook hands.

"Well, come on in. You don't want to be out in the hot sun—you'll be fried by the time you walk in if you stay out any longer," Ben said as he led Pete and Miguel into the cabin.

When Pete entered the cabin, he was astonished because the inside was ten times larger than the outside was.

"Whoa!" Pete yelled out unwittingly. He wasn't expecting to walk in to such a large area.

"The government used an enlargement charm to allow me to have more space. They can't keep me out here without giving me what I want," Ben said, laughing.

Ben led Pete and Miguel into a smaller room, one the size that Pete pictured the entire cabin when he first walked through the door.

"Now, why have you brought such a young boy here? And please don't say what I think you're going to say," Ben said while sitting down behind a desk that was in the room.

Pete sat down next to Miguel in a chair that was right next to the desk as well. "I think he might be the Emerald Prince," Miguel said to Ben.

Ben looked at Miguel then at Pete with a serious look in his eyes. "Are you positive? He's just a boy," Ben said.

"Show him the necklace, Pete," Miguel ordered.

Pete lifted the necklace from inside his shirt, revealing it to Ben.

"My dear God, is that truly it?" Ben asked, surprised. Ben got up from his seat and came around the desk to look at the necklace more closely.

"He's the offspring of the great George Winfield. The last holder of the necklace," Miguel told Ben.

"Oh, yes, I can see him in you. Your father was a great man. I'm so sorry you never got to meet him," Ben said while looking into Pete's eyes.

"Miguel, how do you know that the necklace isn't a fake?" Ben questioned.

"I have seen it take Pete on one of its journeys through time," Miguel replied.

"Really, then what did it look like when he returned?" Ben questioned again.

"There was a flash of light and an explosion of green fire that erupted where the light flashed. Then Pete appeared through the newly made flame like he was teleporting but in a different way," Miguel answered Ben once again.

"There's only one way to find out if the necklace is truly real. Let its owner use the necklace's power," Ben said while looking at Pete. Ben got up and headed for the door saying, "Let's go outside and see."

Miguel got up, and so did Pete. They followed Ben out of the cabin and onto the sandy beach that was in front. When Pete got there, Ben pulled out a wand from inside of his pocket and whipped it toward Pete. A bolt of red light shot out of the wand and hit Pete straight in the chest, causing him to fly back and land on the ground. The necklace immediately began to glow green. Pete got up with a sense that he had gained new strength and pulled out his wand unconsciously.

Pete started toward Ben as Ben shot another curse at him. This time the curse hit a force field surrounding Pete. The curse spun around Pete and then shot toward Ben, just missing him as he jumped out of the way. Sand from the beach began to blow toward Ben.

Pete began to control the new dramatic power that had erupted in him as the necklace stopped glowing. The sand stopped blowing as well.

"Are you crazy? I could have killed you!" Pete yelled at Ben.

"I have proved that the necklace is real. That's all I wanted to know. To be able to get the necklace's power raging, the owner, along with the necklace, need to be tormented with and annoyed for a longer period of time. Nothing would have happened unless I kept shooting spells at you," Ben said while walking toward Pete and Miguel.

"Now it is more likely you are the Emerald Prince," Miguel told Pete.

Chapter Twenty

"Why is it so important that you find the Emerald Prince anyway?" Pete asked while following Miguel and Ben back to the cabin.

"There's a lot you need to know," Ben began. "I'm sure Miguel has told you a lot already?" Ben asked Pete.

"Yes, he has told me about the almighty one sending the element embedded in my necklace to create mutants. He has told me about the secret messenger that brought wizardry, and he told me about the almighty one's plan to end the war between good and evil," Pete said while looking at Ben.

"Yes, that is part of it. Did he tell you about the millions of lives that were affected by wizardry, mutants, and the element?" Ben asked Pete.

"Yeah, he told me peoples' lives were changed when the element hit the world's core," Pete answered.

"Thousands of people died, thousands developed diseases, and thousands became mutants at the split second the element hit the core. Also during this time, there was already a war going on between good and evil. The almighty one sent the element to the world to try to gain strength in his armies. One important part of all of this is that the people who died from the element hitting the world became part of the almighty one's army in heaven," Ben said while listening to Pete's question.

"How is that an important part?" Pete asked.

"It is said when the chosen one enters the war between good and evil, the almighty one will send an army for him to control. There wouldn't be enough people here on our world to serve as soldiers," Ben told Pete.

"Why wouldn't there be enough people here on our world?" Pete questioned.

"Evil has overtaken most of the mutants and wizards. The almighty one needs to send in the army of heaven, which consists of all of the mutants and wizards that have ever died. That number is far greater than the number the evil side has," Ben answered.

"What else do I need to know about me being the Emerald Prince?" Pete asked.

"Nothing more except you're on your way to the craziest trip of your life. The only thing left you have to do now is go to the falling of the seven courts," Ben explained.

Miguel had moved into the other room without Pete even noticing.

"Where and what is the falling of the seven courts?" Pete asked while turning around to look at Miguel but finding only an empty chair.

"Miguel, the boy doesn't even know about the seven courts?" Ben asked, aggravated.

Miguel came back into the room now and answered Ben, "No. Pete has no idea about them more than likely. He has just found out about all of this. So you will need to explain them to him too."

"The seven courts are located in the middle of the Great Ocean. The courts are located on an island. They are at the very location where the element hit the world and entered into the world's core. The courts were designed to keep different parts of the world safe. There was one court for each landmass, one for each continent. The courts were made up of seven people. Each had one special power that resembled their continent. Each leader was named with a special name that started with either queen or king and ended in the name of the continent. Queen Issia controlled the power of the weather. She was nicknamed Mother of Nature. Queen Akira controlled the power of water. Queen Citrica controlled the power of ice. King North Meric controlled the power of the land. King Prore' controlled the power of wind. King South Meric controlled the power of fire, and King Liatral controlled the power of flight," Ben said then hesitated briefly.

"Each one of the courts possessed a necklace just like the one you wear around your neck, but their necklaces didn't have even half of the power of the green-eyed necklace. Each necklace was a different color. They were the colors blue for water, silver for ice, red for fire, brown for land, gold for weather, purple for wind, and yellow for flight. Each one of these necklaces was created from the element embedded in the green-eyed necklace," Ben explained.

"How were the other necklaces created from the green-eyed necklace's element? Who made them?" Pete asked.

"They were created by the person who found the green-eyed necklace, the first one to have it. He was the one who wanted to create the courts. Therefore he had control over them," Ben answered.

"Who was it?" Pete questioned.

"Well, it would have to be one of your ancestors. The green-eyed necklace only works for those related to its first owner," Ben answered Pete.

"So you're telling me one of my ancestors ran the courts?" Pete asked.

"Yes," Ben said.

"What was his name?" Pete questioned.

"That we do not know. No one ever knew his name. His nickname was the Emerald King, and that is why you shall be called the Emerald Prince," Ben explained to Pete.

After Ben explained that to Pete, there was a loud noise outside of the cabin. Miguel got up and looked out of the window, immediately backing away from it.

"They're here," Miguel said.

"Who?" Pete asked.

"King Falcort and his followers," Ben said, answering Pete for Miguel.

"You must leave," Ben ordered Miguel and Pete. "They're here for me."

"Why would they be here for you?" Pete asked Ben.

"I'm the only one who knows how to stop King Falcort. And he has found out where the government has been hiding me. I have been waiting for them," Ben said in a brave voice.

As Pete sat there waiting to see what would happen, wondering who King Falcort was, the green-eyed necklace that he wore around his neck began to glow. As the necklace glowed, Pete tried to speak to Miguel and ask what was going on, but nothing came out. He kept trying and trying, but nothing happened. The necklace was taking over control of Pete's body.

Chapter Twenty-One

Pete was forced up by the necklace and was walking over to the door to the outside of the cabin. Miguel turned and saw Pete heading toward the door. "Get away from there, Pete!" Pete turned around to reveal to Miguel and Ben that his eyes were glowing.

"The necklace has sensed the presence of the red-eyed necklace. It senses that evil is controlling it. There is no stopping him. The only thing that we can hope for is that Pete controls the power," Ben told Miguel.

Pete still had no control of his body movements; they were controlled by the necklace. Pete walked through the door to the outside, now seeing about a hundred people outside waiting for something to happen. When the crowd of people noticed that Pete had stepped outside, the wizards in the crowd pointed their wands at him.

King Falcort was surveying the surroundings of the building and also eyeing Pete. He scanned Pete from the distance, noticing that Pete didn't appear to be any problem, but he would soon be wrong.

"Kill the boy," King Falcort said to his followers.

The crowd of people, which consisted of mutants and wizards, started toward Pete. They reached about forty feet in front of Pete when Pete's arms flew back, creating a force field around him. Pete's arms slashed toward the crowd, throwing the force field at them, causing them to fly back. Pete's body turned toward where King Falcort was and began to walk toward him. Falcort now realized that Pete was a problem and created a force field of his own and sent it toward Pete. When Falcort's force field hit Pete, nothing happened. His force field wasn't strong enough.

"You shall not break the laws of the courts anymore. You shall be punished for your guilt. The punishment shall be death," Pete said but in a different voice. The voice was deeper and more serious. The voice also had an echo to it.

After Pete said that, King Falcort pulled out his wand and began shooting curses at Pete. None of the curses hit Pete. There was another force field that surrounded Pete that didn't let the curses through. Pete raised his hands into the air unwillingly. The necklace was still in control, and a ball-shaped object protruded from thin air and began to shine a blinding light. King Falcort knew what he was dealing with. And when he saw Pete protrude the blinding light from in between his hands, he knew he had to leave.

King Falcort flicked his wand toward his followers, causing them to disappear into black smoke. The ball of light that formed in between Pete's hands began to flash, and what looked like lightning bolts began to strike all around Pete from the ball of light. Pete moved his hands down until they were pointing at King Falcort. And at that instant, the ball of light exploded, sending a wave of light toward King Falcort, burning everything in its path.

As the light came toward King Falcort, he was able to escape with a flash of red light. With King Falcort gone, the wave of light traveled out into the waters of the ocean, turning the water into nothing but steam. The outer parts of the blast caught the edge of the trees that were behind Ben's cabin. When the wave of light hit the trees, it immediately tore them apart. Then Pete finally gained control over the necklace after sending the blast at King Falcort.

After gaining control, he lost strength throughout his body. He fell to the ground, awaiting his body to heal. Ben and Miguel came running out of the cabin after seeing no one was there anymore and ran over to where Pete was. When they reached Pete, his body had healed, and he was just coming back to his normal state.

"Pete, are you all right?" Ben asked.

"Yeah, what happened?" Pete answered then questioned.

"The necklace seemed to have felt the presence of the red-eyed necklace. The red-eyed necklace is in the hands of the evilest mutant sorcerer to ever walk this world. It reacted strongly because it has been longing to find it," Ben told Pete.

"Oh," Pete said, surprised.

Ben and Miguel got Pete back on his feet and started toward the cabin to get back inside before anything else happened. As they walked up the steps to the cabin, there was a flash of light in the sky. They all looked up noticing, a bolt of light shooting toward them. They all jumped off from the steps, down into the cushioning grass on the ground. The bolt of light, just missing them, crashed into Ben's cabin, causing it to ignite into flames. The green-eyed necklace began to glow again, but this time it wasn't the necklace controlling Pete; it was Pete controlling the necklace and its power.

Pete really had no idea how to work the power of the necklace. But when he felt the necklace start to react again, he wasn't going to be controlled; he was going to control it. The sudden control of the necklace's power just happened, and Pete had no idea how he had gained control.

Pete got up and raised his hands into the air, creating another force field like the necklace did earlier. The force field rose into the air, covering the burning cabin and a few of its surroundings. Pete turned around and began to walk toward the cabin, keeping most of his attention on keeping the force field strong. When Pete reached the cabin, he pushed the door open and stepped into a blast of raging hot flames.

As he walked through the flames, he felt the burning of the fire on his skin. But that didn't stop him. He needed to put the flames out; he had to save Ben's cabin. He began thinking that over and over. And finally the necklace did something for him. Around the outside of his body where the fire was burning him turned a greenish color. Then his whole body began to glow as green flames. The newly made green fire acted like a shield just like the force field had when Pete was attacking King Falcort.

Now Pete raised his hands into the air, still thinking over and over, *I have to put this fire out*. As he thought that for a moment, the answer came to him. The green flames that surrounded Pete blasted out from around him and turned the flames that covered the house green also. This meant that Pete had full control of what the fire would do now.

Pete did exactly what he intended to do: he put the fire out. The raging fire that was now green weakened until it just surrounded Pete's body. And eventually it went out completely.

The blast of light that caused the cabin to ignite into fire shattered the glass of the windows and caused the furniture in the house to go on end. Ben's cabin was a total mess now. The walls were black, the siding was charred black from the heat and smoke of the fire, and the good thing was the cabin was still standing, and part of it wasn't damaged at all. Pete went into the part that hadn't been damaged and grabbed his school bag. He was happy that finally he had controlled the power of the necklace. But then he remembered that he had created a force field outside to protect the cabin from any more damage and that it might not be there anymore.

Pete hurried outside only to find that the force field was still there but weakened. He gained back the control of the necklace and strengthened the force field, but what he had just done was too late. He looked out into the ocean to notice something that he never thought could happen. He had no idea that any such wizard or mutant could do anything like what he had just noticed. King Falcort was floating up in the air about one hundred yards out with his hands pointing down at the water. He was glowing red as he sent a large wave of water toward the island where Pete was. Pete only noticed the wave when it was fifty yards away. Total destruction was imminent.

CHAPTER TWENTY-TWO

Pete sat there for a moment in shock but soon came back into his normal state of mind. As he came out of shock he heard someone yelling, "Pete, get over here!" It was Miguel.

Pete turned toward where the voice came from and saw Ben and Miguel standing behind the trees that were by the side of the cabin. It was too late for Pete to try to reach them. The only thing he could do now was try to stop the wave of water.

The green-eyed necklace began to glow bright as usual as Pete began to control its powers. Pete created the strongest force field that he could muster and sent it out toward the wave. The wave came crashing up onto the beach, tearing the ground apart. The wave was suddenly stopped by Pete's force field, which acted like a large wall. The water hit the force field and immediately spun around it, crashing into the trees that surrounded the cabin. Finally the water stopped coming. Pete lowered the force field, noticing that King Falcort was nowhere to be seen.

Pete felt exhausted but stayed strong and stood there like nothing had happened. His body healed within moments, but he hadn't hurt as bad as all the other times he had used the green-eyed necklace's powers. Pete was finally being able to use the power without side effects.

"I think it's time for us to leave," Miguel whispered in Pete's ear.

When Pete heard him say that, he felt Miguel's hand grab onto his arm. There was a flash of white light as Pete, Miguel, and Ben disappeared from the now-abandoned island. They were flying through what seemed like a cloud again and appeared in a different place. They were back inside Goodrick's, but it was night, and no one was awake.

They crept through the darkened school as Miguel led Pete and Ben toward a large archway that was near the main office of the school. The center of the archway wasn't opened or filled with huge doors; instead it was filled in with bricks. Miguel took out his wand and tapped one of the bricks. He said something under his breath that Pete couldn't make out into words. After Miguel said that, the bricks began to twist and turn as they made a new, smaller passageway that they could walk into.

"Follow me," Miguel said. Pete and Ben followed him down a hallway until they reached a door that said, "Mathew Goodrick, Principal." Miguel knocked on the door and said, "Matt, you need to get out here. There are some very important things we need to talk about."

As the three of them stood outside the headmaster's door, they heard someone walking toward the door from the inside. The door's handle twisted, and the door opened. From behind the door appeared Goodrick.

"Why in the world are you waking me up at three o'clock in the morning? This better be good," Goodrick said grumpily.

"Oh, I wish it were something good. But I'm afraid we have little time to let the mutant, wizardry, and the mortal governments know about what happened tonight," Miguel began to explain.

Goodrick noticed that Ben was standing in the doorway behind Miguel and put two and two together to realize what happened.

"King Falcort found Ben," Goodrick said, assuming.

"Yes, and King Falcort tried to kill all of us. He used one of his favorite tactics. He sent a tidal wave at us to try to drown us. It was a good thing that we had young Pete there with us. He saved all of our lives," Miguel finished explaining.

"Oh, well, that's good. What kind of power do you have Pete?" Goodrick asked Pete.

"Uh ..." Pete began.

"He's telekinetic," Miguel lied for Pete.

"We need to send a letter hog to the governments. King Falcort might still be traveling in the Teleport galaxy," Ben said, interrupting Goodrick's conversation with Miguel and now Pete.

"Teleport galaxy? King Falcort destroyed the station that tracks the galaxy just a few days ago. They won't have any luck looking there," Goodrick answered Ben.

"How come I didn't get a message about this?" Ben asked angrily. "After all, I'm the one who lived out in the middle of nowhere, where it was supposed to be the hardest place to get to," Ben said angrily again.

"Well, I'm not the one who is supposed to let you know about what has happened," Goodrick said back to Ben sarcastically.

"Get out of here. We need to let the governments know," Miguel said while pushing Ben back out into the hallway.

Miguel went over to the principal's desk and grabbed a piece of paper and a pen. He wrote on the paper,

> We have sighted King Falcort at Ben's cabin. They attacked us. He knew where we had hidden Ben. We are at Goodrick's now, so we are safe. Take immediate action on trying to fix the Teleport galaxy. He could still be there. Report back with information on finding him.
>
> —Miguel Johnson

After Miguel wrote the letter, he pulled out his wand from the inside of his pocket. He tapped the sheet of paper and said, "Trio-copiet." When the tip of the wand hit the paper, it created a spark. It looked like the paper lit fire, but what appeared to be flames rolled off the paper and turned into two more of the same exact piece of paper. Then he tapped the first one and said, "Hog-mailer." The paper began to wrinkle and take the shape of a small pig. He did the same to the other two, and they too turned into small pigs.

Miguel went back to the first pig that he created, and it asked him, "Where would you like the letter to be delivered?"

Miguel answered the pig, "To the president of the mortal government." He went to the next pig, and it asked him the same question, and he answered, "To the president of the mutant government." Then Miguel answered the last pig that asked the same question, "To the president of the wizardry government."

After Miguel answered each pig on where to deliver the letters, the pigs leapt up into the air and shot out of Goodrick's window toward their destinations. When the three pigs reached the outside, they shot like bullets across the dark sky, disappearing within a few seconds.

Chapter Twenty-Three

The pigs reached the presidents of each of the three governments. They arrived at the headquarters of each government at night. When the pigs arrived, they awoke the presidents. The pigs turned back into the letters to allow the presidents to read them. Each president read their letter and responded back.

The letter hogs returned one by one until they were all there with the responses from each president. To Miguel's surprise, each one of the letters read the same thing:

> There is no way of finding him. It is impossible. The only thing that shall solve this is the force of war.
> President...
> ...Luco
> ...Jamison
> ...Carmin

"War. Their only way of solving this issue is to go to war with King Falcort and his army?" Miguel questioned out loud after reading each letter.

"Matt, did you know anything about this?" Miguel asked Goodrick.

"Of course I did. A war is the only solution. We fight King Falcort and show him who really is the most powerful."

"Why didn't you ever tell us any of this?" Ben asked Goodrick.

"It's confidential and only between the presidents and the seven courts."

"If it is only between the courts and the presidents, then how did you find out?"

"One of my dear friends is on the courts," Goodrick answered with a nervous look appearing on his face.

"And who is that?"

"That doesn't matter to you, does it now!" Goodrick yelled. "Now leave before I call the government on you. All of you leave!" Goodrick yelled at them all this time.

Ben stormed out of the room angry. Miguel told Pete to follow. Pete left the room, following Ben. Miguel soon came out from the doorway with the huge archway surrounding it.

Ben turned to Miguel and looked straight into his eyes and said, "That man is crazy, Miguel. He has no idea what King Falcort can do. If we go to war, innocent lives will be taken. It could mean the end of the world." Ben began to pace back and forth in front of the large archway. "I guess the only thing we can do is call an emergency meeting with the courts," Ben said at last after pacing back and forth for a while.

"How can we do that?" Pete asked, confused. How were they supposed to call an emergency meeting with such an important group of people?

"You're the new leader of the courts. Didn't we tell you this?" Ben said sarcastically.

"No, we never told him. We only told him that the first conqueror of the green-eyed necklace ran the courts. We never told him that the reign went with the holder of the necklace," Miguel explained to Ben.

"So you're telling me that I am the new leader of the courts?" Pete asked nervously.

"Yes, yes, you are," Ben answered.

"Why do we have to call an emergency meeting with the courts anyway?" Pete questioned once again in the same nervous voice.

"Each one of the courts has their own armies. We need to gather together and come up with a plan to take King Falcort out along with his army," Ben explained while looking straight at Pete. "Now, we don't have all the time in the world, so we must get going. Lead the way please." Ben said while nodding to Miguel.

"Follow me," Miguel said as he walked and turned around the corner away from the large archway.

Miguel was walking fast as they went past the main office and turned down to the same hallway that Miguel and Pete had gone down to go to see Ben. It was the forbidden hallway that they weren't allowed in during school. As they reached the huge archway, with huge wooden doors, Miguel said something under his breath while flicking his wand at the two smaller doors. This time Pete made it out to be "sunshine battle."

The doors swung open, and they entered into the large room. Pete noticed the small-looking closet hole in the wall that they traveled by before to get to Ben's but looked ahead of where they were walking and saw something he didn't notice before. There, ahead of them on a large platform, stood an arc that took up a quarter of the space in the room. It was made of golden marble, and moonlight reflected off it, which shined through the large window up onto the back wall of the room.

They were heading up the stairs to the top of the platform. They reached the top, and Miguel said, "Wait right here. It will just be a moment."

Miguel walked alongside of the platform over to where a large marble post stuck up out of the platform. On the top of the post was something in the shape of a cylinder with a hole in the center. The thing on top of the post was a different color; it looked like a large diamond.

Miguel waved his wand in midair as a large crystal appeared about the size of the length and width of the hole in the cylinder-shaped object on top of the marble post. Miguel grabbed the large crystal and pointed his wand at it and said, "To the falling of the courts," and when he said that, the crystal began to shine a bright white color.

Miguel put the crystal into the hole of the object on top of the post. The large diamond-looking object began to shine all the colors of a rainbow, and the large arc that stood in the middle of the large platform was filled with a cloudy silver substance and began to shine as well.

Miguel, by the time the arc began to fill with the silver substance, had walked back over to where Pete stood, amazed, and Ben stood, looking excited.

"Shall we go then?" Miguel asked.

"After you, Pete," Ben said.

Pete instinctively knew what to do. He walked toward the bright light that now engulfed the inside of the arc and seemed to have been engulfed by the light as well. He seemed to be traveling through an empty space. It was a warm, happy feeling.

As the feeling seemed to last forever, he saw at last the bright light dim and what seemed to him to be a new world emerging in front of him.

Chapter Twenty-Four

He was standing on a rough, rocky surface that was on the edge of a large cliff that overlooked the huge, dark Great Ocean. No sooner than after he realized what was surrounding him, two flashes of light flashed on each side of him as Miguel and Ben appeared.

"Well, here we are. The Land of the Seven Courts," Ben said while walking away from the side of the cliff toward a half-standing tower. Pete and Miguel followed.

As they walked through the darkness, Pete heard different sounds from what he thought to be animals. They reached a large forest that led all the way up to the half-standing tower. The sun was just coming over large mountains that Pete could see in the distance farther beyond the tower. As they entered the forest, the new sunlight that was shining over the land was immediately blocked out by the canopy that lined the top of the thick trees.

Ben pulled out his wand, and so did Miguel. Pete followed suit. Ben pointed his wand out in front and whispered, "Lighten factula." The leaf buds of his wand began to glow as a beam of light lit up the dirt trail that led through the forest.

As they walked for what seemed to be hours, the strange animal noises got louder, and they seemed to get closer. Finally, after what seemed hours, the trail ended. But there was nowhere to go. It was a dead end.

"Well, isn't this just great," Pete blurted out.

"Shh..." Ben turned and mouthed to Pete.

No sooner than after Ben told Pete to be quiet, the trees surrounding them became loud with the animal noises.

"Who dares to walk in the Forest of the Courts?" someone asked from the shadows of the trees.

"We're trying to get to the courts," Pete said aloud.

Ben and Miguel both turned around and gave Pete a nasty look.

Pete just shrugged and said back, "What else could I say?"

"The courts, why do you need to go there? It is only the one with the key who shall enter, and from what I sense from you three, none of you holds the key," the unknown being asked from the shadows.

As Pete, Ben, and Miguel stood there, the unknown being soon stepped out from the shadows and revealed himself. It was a centaur. He had long, brown hair and was as tall as a draft horse. It wasn't the kind of creature that alarmed them the most though; it was the bow and arrow he had pointed out in front ready to fire at any moment.

"There won't be any need for that," Ben said while raising his wand toward the centaur, shining the light that came from the tip at him.

"I would put that away if I were you," the centaur said while aiming at Ben.

"I will do as I want. Rebe—" Ben started to say.

"No!" Pete yelled.

And as Pete yelled out to stop Ben, he made a force field in between them all and the centaur. The centaur was alarmed and let the arrow go. The arrow flew toward Ben but was disintegrated by the power of the force field. The arrow turned to dust.

When Pete created the force field, his necklace came out from under his shirt and began to glow as he controlled it. The centaur saw the necklace and backed away from them.

"I'm terribly sorry, Great One," the centaur said while kneeling down with his two front hooves in a bow toward Pete.

Out from the shadows where the centaur first came from came other centaurs along with other creatures of the forest. As they came out from inside the forest, they all began to bow toward Pete, just as the centaurs did.

"What is going on?" Pete asked while enlarging the force field so it protected them on all angles.

"It's all right, Pete. They know who you are. They won't hurt us," Miguel explained.

"I didn't mean to bring harm to you in any way, Great One. My senses have been a little off. I should have noticed your presence. After all, you look just like your father," the first centaur said while getting up.

All of the other creatures followed after him and got up.

"How did you know my father?" Pete questioned.

"He was the last owner of the necklace you wear around your neck. He was the ruler of these lands. And he chose me to be the protector of them. He was the last leader of the courts. Everyone knew who he was," the centaur answered Pete.

"Pete, we don't have time to get to know the centaur or about the past just yet. We have to get up to the tower," Ben said with an urging voice.

"Show us the way..." Pete said to the centaur, motioning him to give Pete his name.

"William, my name is William," the centaur named William said. "Follow me," William ordered as he walked toward a large tree that was in the center of the end of the trail.

When Pete and the other two reached the tree, they saw a large knot in the center that was at chest high to Pete. William pushed the knot in with his palm, and as he did that, the knot began to shine a bright-blue color.

"Just stand in front of the tree, Great One. It's the only safe entrance into the tower," William told Pete while backing out of the way.

Pete looked over at Miguel and Ben and gave them a questioning look.

"Go ahead. It's all right," Miguel said while answering Pete's speechless question.

Pete walked over in front of the tree and stood there with the light from the knot shining into the eye of his necklace.

The light shined onto the necklace, causing the necklace to glow. And as the necklace glowed, the knot came back out and caused a vein-shaped cut to form down the center of the tree and down into the roots.

As Pete stood there, the knot eventually disappeared, and the vein-shaped cut opened up, revealing a large doorway that revealed a long tunnel that had lots of twists and turns. The necklace stopped glowing, and they began to follow William down the long tunnel that led them to their destination of the falling of the seven courts.

CHAPTER TWENTY-FIVE

As William led the way down the long tunnel, torches along the walls of the tunnel ignited themselves, illuminating the tunnel so they could see. It seemed like more endless hours of walking, but soon after Pete began to get tired of walking, he saw the end of the tunnel. At the end stood stairs that led up to what Pete soon knew to be the inside of the half-standing tower.

They walked up the stairs and ended up in a very large room with no ceiling; the top of the tower obviously had been destroyed. The tower was much larger than Pete had expected. Lined in front of where they were standing, Pete could make out that two thirds of the circular structures used to have stairs and benches. The hard-to-make-out stairs and benches lined the still-standing walls all the way up as high as the walls stood. Pete knew now this used to be some kind of meeting hall for the courts.

They stood above the seats that lined the walls that overlooked the whole room.

"What happened to this place?" Pete asked.

"It was destroyed back during the last war. Back when the courts used to meet here. The only place where they should meet," William answered.

"How are we going to call a meeting in a place that is in ruins? And how many people are in the courts anyway? There are seats here for about three hundred," Pete questioned while looking around the large room.

"That's where you come in, Pete. I take it that you have the book here with you?" Ben asked him.

"Yes. It's right here," Pete said while pulling the book with the large green eye on the front of it from his backpack. "What am I going to do?" Pete asked.

"In the book should be a section that tells what happened to the courts. It should give you a riddle that, when read out loud, will rebuild the courts, as long as you read it here," Ben explained. "And you're going to read the riddle aloud since you're the only one able to read the book and its contents," Ben said while answering Pete's question about what Pete was going to do.

"How in the world am I going to find a section just for that? This book must have four thousand pages in it," Pete asked once again.

"Just tell the book to find it for you. Try telling it to find the falling of the seven courts," Ben said, again getting aggravated.

Pete opened the book and said very clearly, "Find me the falling of the seven courts section."

And to Pete's surprise, the book's pages turned very fast until it reached a page toward the end of the book.

The symbols twisted and turned into letters that Pete could read and revealed in the center of one of the pages a picture of what Pete figured to be the tower they stood in back when it stood strong.

Pete began to read it aloud:

"A tower that once stood tall and strong lost its strength to one who wanted power for too long.

"She withstood the battle until the very end even though her master had met his end.

"The remains that still stand here shall be rebuilt at one request: that her new master shall take in its bequest.

"The dust and devastation that is left over shall turn into what was standing here once before and nothing moreover.

"I shall take my bequest and rebuild her tall and strong

"This shall be the only request, and I shall do nothing wrong."

At the very moment Pete finished reading the riddle, the ground began to shake as the dust that was around the tower flew up into the air and began to circle the broken walls. As the dust rose into the air, Pete fell to the ground as images began to shoot through his mind while he still looked at the book. The book's pages began to turn rapidly just like they did before. This time the book gave Pete all the information it held inside of it.

CHAPTER TWENTY-SIX

Large pillars shot from underground and met together, creating what was soon to be a cathedral ceiling. New brick walls began to rise from the top of the broken walls and encased the newly made pillars to form the shape of the tower in the book that Pete was holding. Large windows formed from the dust in the center between each pair of pillars all the way to the top while the new brick walls formed around them, holding them in their place.

The dust remains swirled around the broken tops of the stairs and benches, creating new ones. The stairs had separated the benches into seven sections. And above the sections small suites were created, overlooking the rest of the room. The cracks and craters that scattered the floor below were filled in, revealing a newly made floor.

In the center of the floor appeared a large golden chair with green emeralds that layered it. At the top of the cathedral ceiling sprouted a stem of lights that grew into a large, crystal plant that lit up the entire room. And large wooden doors grew through the brick walls on every right angle.

William, Ben, and Miguel hadn't noticed that Pete had fallen to the ground after he read the riddle. They were too distracted by what was going on around them.

After the tower had been rebuilt, Miguel noticed Pete on the floor, looking into the pages of the book as they turned rapidly.

"Pete! What's going on?" Miguel yelled, running over to him.

William and Ben turned around, noticing Pete also, and ran over to his side. Ben hurried and grabbed Miguel by the arm to stop him from doing anything to stop what was happening to Pete.

"What are you doing? Let go of me," Miguel said while trying to reach Pete.

"It's all right. This is what's supposed to happen," Ben told Miguel to calm him down.

Miguel stopped trying to get away from Ben as he released Miguel's arm.

Pete sat there, transfixed, while looking into the book. The book's pages were turning rapidly. Pete's eyes began to glow green with the pages of the book.

The book kept Pete transfixed for a little longer until the pages stopped turning and it shut itself. It revealed on the front the green-eyed necklace glowing, and they also saw that Pete's necklace was glowing as well. When the necklaces stopped glowing, Pete was returned to his original state of mind.

Pete looked down at the book moments later, and his head had a severe pain shoot through it, causing him to scream. Pete's scream echoed throughout the entire tower. The pain finally stopped, and Pete spoke his first words after being transfixed. "What's going on?"

Pete had spoken in a weak voice, making Miguel even more nervous.

Miguel and Ben hurried over to Pete and got him up onto his feet.

"It won't be long until you feel normal," Ben said to Pete.

"Why did the book do that to me?" Pete asked, ignoring what Ben had said.

"You gave the book your word," Ben answered him.

"I never gave my word to anything," Pete told Ben.

"Did you not pay attention to the riddle at all? You said at the end, 'I shall take my bequest,' which means you gave your word on taking your inheritance," Ben explained.

"Okay, now it makes sense," Pete said, sort of chuckling.

Pete now walked out into the center in front of the golden chair and said, while pointing his wand out toward the center of the room, "Courts, I call this meeting to order." As he said that, a silver force field protruded from the tip of his wand and crashed into the walls of the room and exploded across the grounds of the courts and throughout the entire world.

"What's going on, Ben? What just happened to Pete, and how did he know how to call the courts to meet?" Miguel asked, turning to Ben.

"Pete was informed of everything known to the magical community. He knows everything the book held in it. It contained every moment in time since it was created. It showed him the things that happened in the past that led to what's happening today. The book gave him all the tools to defeat evil and allow peace to run throughout our world. His maturity level went from a teenager to a grown man." Ben finished while turning away from Miguel.

Miguel felt better now that he was filled in. He had no idea what was going on until now.

Pete was standing in the same spot as when he called the courts, but now he had his wand lowered. He stood there, waiting for something to happen. And as he stood waiting, the newly made benches swirled amid flaming, fiery flashes. And as the ashes settled, it created people. The flashes of fire were the colors of each of the courts.

People were appearing all across the room. They were filling the seats that layered the newly made walls. And above, in the suites that overlooked the entire room, flashed a single color in each of them: blue, silver, gold, brown, purple, and yellow. Each suite held the leader for one of the seven courts. All of the leaders and courts were there except for the red court. All the people looked around at each other, surprised to be there and very confused.

After the flashes of light ceased and people stopped emanating from flames, Pete began to talk. His voice was echoing loudly enough so that everyone in the room could hear him.

"Dear people of the courts, I come here in front of you today to introduce myself. I am your new leader and guider, Pete Winfield, the son of George Winfield."

Everyone began to talk across the hall after Pete had said who he was.

"Silence! There's much to discuss," Pete said with an ordering voice. "We all know that there is betrayal among our world today and that the person leading this betrayal must be stopped," Pete said while looking all across the room. "King Falcort and his armies shall not walk in triumph anymore. We shall take them out with our most powerful weapons and end the war between good and evil. We shall bring peace to our world after the long past fifteen years," Pete finished while being interrupted by someone else with a loud echoing voice. The voice was coming from the female leader of gold court.

"How do you know anything about what has happened? You look only fifteen years old yourself."

"And you're correct, but I have received the necessary information needed to finish the war. You all know of the book. I have read its contents and come before you today to tell you that I am the chosen one—the Emerald Prince," Pete said while holding up the book in front of the crowd.

The eye in the center of the book began to glow. And that gave the answer to all of the leaders in the suites above their courts. The book would only glow if the chosen one had read it; all the courts had known that.

"Is that enough information to show you that I'm telling you the truth? If it is, everyone who agrees say aye." There was a loud echo of people saying "aye." "Everyone who disagrees say 'nay.'" No one in the crowd said "nay." "Then I shall ask for a bond between the courts," Pete said while pointing his wand into the air. A jet of green light shot out from the tip and exploded at the top of the room into a large green eye.

The leaders of the six courts shot jets of light of the color of their court as well, causing the large green eye to change into all the colors of the courts, all but the color red.

"Now that we are on the same page, I would like to ask all of you to get your armies ready for battle. The war begins tomorrow night," Pete said. But the crowd jumped up off their seats, yelling because they disagreed with what Pete had just said.

"We cannot go to war with such short notice. Most of our soldiers are at their homes with their families. They won't want to leave to go to war," the leader of the blue courts said.

"Soldiers should always be ready, as I am sure they are. When they join a military force such as we have here, they sign their lives over to the force. The soldiers have their agreements to fight for the courts whenever needed. And tomorrow is the day the war must begin before any other innocent lives are taken. Call your armies here tomorrow at noon. We leave here at five," Pete finished while sitting down in the golden chair. "Are there any questions from the court leaders? Because, to my understanding, my father gave you the information that today was to come, and he told you what would need to happen."

George told the courts they had to call their armies and fight whenever the new leader of all the courts came. George told them they had to do whatever it took to win the battle. The bad thing was the courts only knew that they had to call their armies; they didn't know what they were going to be battling. They had no idea what size army King Falcort would have.

Chapter Twenty-Seven

Pete adjourned the meeting and sent the entire court home. He was amazed how well the courts listened to him. The information that he got from the book would prove to the courts that he was telling the truth. He couldn't believe it. He was overwhelmed with all the information he had gotten. He tried to sort it all out in his head, but there was so much information. With all of the knowledge Pete had gained from the book, he now had full control over the necklace's power. And part of its power was to locate all of the other necklaces.

"Pete, I have to tell you that I was wrong about you being too young. You seem like you know enough to do the job. But let me ask you: are you ready?" Ben asked Pete.

"Yeah, I can do it. After all, I'm immortal. I can't die," Pete said back to Ben.

"Don't think for one second that there aren't ways for you to not exist in the state you are in," Ben said to Pete in a serious tone. "King Falcort knows things that you didn't get from the book. He knows things that no one can even imagine," Ben said again in the same serious voice.

William had gone back out into the forest to protect the lands. Pete, Ben, and Miguel were going to stay there for the night while Pete drew out the plan for the attack from the information that the book gave him. He located King Falcort's whereabouts while coming up with the plan.

As Pete located King Falcort, he soon found out that Falcort was at a location that was very visible. Pete looked deeper into Falcort's whereabouts and saw that he was at Goodrick's. He had taken over the school. He also sensed that Falcort's followers had taken over the streets of the Xertan colony. He couldn't tell if they had taken hostages of the citizens that lived there.

"He's at Goodrick's in Xerta," Pete yelled. "King Falcort has taken over the school," Pete said again.

Ben and Miguel were over on two beds, resting, thinking of their own plans about what to do when they heard what Pete said.

"Impossible. There's no way he could have gotten into Goodrick's," Ben said while walking over to Pete.

"Yes, there is," Miguel said while getting up too. "We use a separate teleport galaxy station than the one used for everyone else. It's possible that he found the other station and got into the school," Miguel explained.

"What would he want with the school?" Ben asked out loud while meaning to talk to himself.

"It was my fault," Pete began. "King Falcort still has his necklace, and he heard me when I called for the meeting. He knew what was coming and took over the school to try to stop us. He is probably going to use the kids as hostages," Pete finished while feeling scared all of sudden, worried about Lucy.

"Your father destroyed the connection between the necklace's powers and Falcort's control years ago. King Falcort couldn't have known about the meeting," Ben said.

"He was wearing the necklace back at your house when he attacked us. He used its powers to create the wave that almost killed us," Pete explained to Ben.

"That wasn't the necklace's power that was attacking us. King Falcort's mutant ability is that he can move things with his mind. He's telekinetic," Ben said to Pete.

"Then explain why he was glowing red, the color of the necklace, when he created the wave," Pete ordered Ben, getting angry.

"That I cannot explain totally, but I think after having control over the necklace for so long, he turns that color because that's what he usually turned when using his mutant powers," Ben explained.

"That might be, but we need to get going. Whatever is going on, we know the red-eyed necklace has no power. George destroyed it a long time ago," Miguel said, interrupting Pete and Ben. "Now if Pete is correct, I think we better go stop King Falcort from doing any harm at Goodrick's," Miguel finished while walking out the door.

Pete and Ben followed him out the door and walked out onto the dark grounds that surrounded the tower.

"I think the platform should be over here if I remember right," Miguel said, shining his light from his wand over at the edge of the dark forest.

Sure enough, over at the edge of the forest was the same kind of platform with the large arc that went across it like the one back at Goodrick's.

Miguel went over to the marble post that stuck out of the floor of the platform and conjured a crystal out of thin air that would take them back to Goodrick's. The same bright light filled the center of the arc, and the three of them stepped through. They all felt the warm, good feeling until they appeared outside of the school along the ocean line. There were no lights on in the school except in the dining hall. It was now just getting light out, and they soon noticed that the entire grounds around the school and colony showed no sign of King Falcort's presence.

CHAPTER TWENTY-EIGHT

Pete had never actually seen the entire grounds during daylight. Surrounding Xerta were large mountains with miles of ocean beyond them. The waters of the ocean reached just below the crests of the mountaintops. The water came high enough to create large waterfalls that fell from the small crevasses in between the mountaintops. The waterfalls fell down into a large pool that also lined the border of the grounds. The water was dark blue, and as the morning sun hit it, the reflection bounced off it, illuminating the hazy clouds above with a blue tint.

Pete couldn't get over the fact that what he saw back at the courts wasn't true. He knew what he saw and sensed trouble going on somewhere near. He had discovered how to use his power at greater lengths. After the book revealed its secrets to him, he knew lots of different spells and different senses he could develop.

"You two stay here. I'm going to have a look around," Pete said while vanishing with a green flash.

"Oh, great, where did he go?" Ben said aloud angrily.

"I'm guessing to have a look around," Miguel answered.

"Oh, very funny. This is no time for fun. A war is about to start," Ben snapped at Miguel.

Pete appeared on top of one of the towers of the school. He could overlook the entire grounds and see for what seemed miles until he viewed the mountains. They seemed much taller than where he was standing, the highest point of the entire colony, even higher than the mountains. The trouble he sensed grew into what he felt as danger. They were all in danger now.

Pete vanished with a flash and appeared in the hallway outside of the main office. No one was awake. He blinked, and his eyes began to glow green as the surroundings of the school walls began to glow a greenish color in Pete's point of view. He could look through the walls.

He could see no one. The door to the dining hall wasn't glowing green at all like all the other walls and doors. Pete walked over to the dining hall doors, and, remembering that this room was the only one with lights on, he pulled out his wand. He pushed open the doors, and as soon as he walked in, he saw in the center of the huge room a large crowd of people bunched together.

All the students and teachers stood in the center of the room, trapped together by a red force field that surrounded them. Pete began to run toward the crowd. He flicked his wand at the force field that surrounded his fellow students and teachers and broke it, causing it to dissolve.

He reached the crowd as the barrier broke, and pointed his wand up into the air and screamed, "Remirrous pretigious!" The tip of his wand let out a green spark, and a balloon in the form of a force field surrounded the crowd now under Pete's control.

"Nobody move!" Pete screamed at the top of his lungs.

Everyone stopped in their tracks. The ones almost out of the newly made protection fell to the ground to stop themselves from hitting the barrier.

As soon as Pete projected the force field, spells began flying from all over the place as figures erupted from black smoke and fire around the room. As the spells flew at the force field that Pete had made, they hit it, but when the spells made contact, they immediately bounced off and flew back into the direction they came from.

The repelled spells were striking one after another of King Falcort's followers, the ones that were too stupid to move out of the way. The spell casting was stopped by a loud voice that echoed through the entire room from the direction of the doors where Pete had entered.

"*Stop!*" King Falcort screamed.

All of his followers ceased at his command and turned toward him and nodded their heads down like he was a god.

Falcort walked over to where Pete and the crowd stood, sheltered under the protection of Pete's force field, but he still stayed back, cautious of what might happen.

"You have finally shown up. I have been waiting for you," Falcort said while looking at Pete.

Pete became nervous, but his braveness over powered his being scared.

"Why hurt innocent people?" Pete asked Falcort while staring back.

"It was the only way to get you here. You fall into traps rather easily," Falcort said back to Pete while still staring at him.

"Trap? Who says this is a trap? I knew perfectly well what might happen," Pete said back to Falcort again. "Why have you come here? What is your purpose in holding these people hostage?" Pete asked, already knowing the answer that Falcort would give him.

"What is a more perfect way to take down the magical governments than from their strongest point?" King Falcort answered Pete.

As Pete stood there in conversation, his mind was taken to another place for a moment. Images began to flash through his mind as the answer came to him, the answer to his longing question of who King Falcort really was. King Falcort's real name was Gabriel. And the new information also told him parts of Falcort's past.

"You know an object is only as strong as its weakest point, Gabriel." King Falcort's face dropped into a nervous look as Pete spoke his name. "You should have taken further precautions on taking us down," Pete said again, making King Falcort more nervous. "But you don't have much time. The clock is ticking, and you might lose your much-sought war," Pete said, now making Falcort angry. "I intend to take you down by your weakest points, and your wish shall be granted, your wish of war," Pete finished while pointing his wand at the see-through glass ceiling above.

King Falcort drew his wand and screamed a curse as a red light of energy shot out the tip of his wand toward

Pete, but it was stopped as Pete's wand shot a bolt of green light up into the ceiling, causing the force field that surrounded Pete and the crowd to blast apart and spread throughout the room. The strength of the force field caused King Falcort and his followers to vanish in black smoke. The bolt of green light shot through the glass like it wasn't there; it didn't break. As the bolt of light shot into the morning light, it exploded with a ripple that went through the entire sky and revealed a large green eye in the form of raging green fire.

CHAPTER TWENTY-NINE

The symbol of an eye being sent up into the air with an explosion was a defense mechanism for each court while in battle. Many different things could be conjured from it if needed. The force field that exploded as Pete conjured the deep magic caused King Falcort and his army to appear outside of the school grounds. They appeared up on top of one of the small mountains. Falcort raged with anger now. Pete gained knowledge of King Falcort's powers after the images flashed before him. It would only be a matter of time before Falcort could break the barrier that Pete created to block him and his army from entering the grounds of the school.

Pete didn't have much time to gather the courts' armies and form an attack plan for the battle ahead. Moreover, he needed to get the students and teachers of Goodrick's to safety.

The crowd around Pete had scattered at the sight of what Pete had just done. They began to back away from him as if they were scared. Most people in the magical world knew what the sign of war was, and the sign hadn't been seen in over ten years. This brought chaos to everyone's mind. No one wanted to be at the school or grounds anymore. Students who learned how to teleport began disappearing after the chaos broke out, and Pete couldn't control them from leaving. He concentrated on a spell that stopped teleportation. It finally came to him as he yelled out, "Stepteleportous!"

The older students who knew how to teleport soon found out they couldn't anymore and became even more scared.

"Everyone, follow me over to the east wing," Pete yelled out.

No one moved toward the east wing. Pete soon noticed that Miguel and Ben came running into the large dining hall.

"Everyone go to the east wing if you want to live! Nobody stays behind," Miguel screamed. After all, Miguel was a teacher at the school.

Everyone followed Miguel in through the large wooden doors that revealed the large arc on the platform in the center of the room. Miguel conjured a large crystal and put it in the hole that went through the marble post that stuck out of the platform. The arc's center began to glow as Miguel directed the students and teachers through the bright light.

Many of the students had no idea what they were going into but went into the bright light anyway. They didn't know what was to happen at the school.

After the large crowd dissipated to just a few of the teachers, there was a loud rumble outside of the castle walls that shook like an earthquake. Pete's newly strengthened senses told him that the courts and their armies had arrived for the battle.

Chapter Thirty

Pete's new knowledge of King Falcort told him that now that he was outside of the school grounds, he could call for, and create, a lot more soldiers. Falcort's powers were stronger now since he wasn't in the presence of the green-eyed necklace.

Pete hurried outside onto the grounds to see the arrival of the courts and their armies. The sky was gray, and the clouds that had protruded around the green eye that was above now circled around the eye like a small hurricane. The wind picked up, and a large whirlpool formed out in the middle of the body of water that surrounded the school grounds. The air grew cold, and then everything seemed to come to a stop.

The outside became quiet until the colors of blue, gold, silver, brown, purple, and yellow flashed before Pete and the others who had followed him outside to see what was happening.

Human figures began sprouting from the ground that looked like plants; water splashed ashore and formed into man-size things that soon came out to be people that had a blue tint to their skin. The clouds above came crashing down atop the tall towers and large walls of the Xertan grounds and protruded humans from their midst. A section of the grounds turned cold and formed a winter scene. From the snow that piled up burst out human-looking creatures of a sort with bright white skin. Up above, in the sky, Pete could see large figures flying down toward the ground, landing in front of the castle doors where Pete stood with Ben and Miguel. And lastly, outlines of humans appeared out of thin air next to the mutants that had just landed.

The plant-people who sprouted from the ground were the Warriors of the Land; they wore swords that hung along their backs with what looked like roots wrapped around together for handles.

The blue-tinted humanlike creatures who splashed out of the water gathered alongside the rest of the armies. They had weapons such as seashells hanging from their waists that were used as explosives, and each one had large rods that had some sort of sharp object on the end for another weapon. This group of warriors was called the Sea Warriors.

The warriors who protruded from the clouds above were the archers for the battle. They were called Wind Carriers. They could make their arrows go to any given spot and curse the arrows to explode on contact.

The white individuals that burst out from the piled-up snow were called Icemen. They wore large belts around their waists that carried explosive objects that looked like snowballs. And they had long spears that were made of everlasting ice hung along their backs.

The mutants who flew down from the sky were the Flight Warriors. They had extra gifts like mutants, such as flame throwing and super strength. They didn't need any such weapon since their gifts were their strongest weapon.

The people who had appeared out of thin air were the Teleporters. They had the abilities like the Flight Warriors. They had the gifts of super strength and also the ability to slow time and attack much faster than other warriors.

As the first of the warriors of the courts appeared from their originations, more of the same kind of each group kept coming. The growing strength of the army didn't stop until the gray clouds above diminished and the sun shined brightly across the entire grounds. The sun and the green eye that shined above were in line with each other. It seemed like the green eye was the sun.

The armies gathered together around Pete, waiting for his command. Pete knew that he now was their commander and soon began to speak but was delayed by the arrival of the leaders of the six courts, who had brought their armies to him. They all appeared with a flash of the color of their court and stood in a straight line with Pete.

"Here today we shall fight for peace. For peace within the courts and the world," Pete paused for a moment, taking in what was before him. There was a feeling in him that couldn't believe what he was doing. It seemed crazy. "You all have trained for this very day for the past thousand years. And today shall be the day that your training pays off." Pete stopped again, recalling his battle plan to himself. "The blue, silver, and brown armies shall take up the front while the others stay back and attack with force from behind." Pete paused for another moment but was stopped this time by something else.

Alongside the mountain where King Falcort and his followers had been exiled, black clouds began to form as King Falcort performed the counter curse to the barrier that kept him from entering the grounds, and he also began to recite the enchantments that would awaken his army.

CHAPTER THIRTY-ONE

The black, vicious clouds swirled with anger as Falcort chanted the counter curse to the barrier. The black clouds Falcort was creating were no ordinary clouds; they were a curse that would allow him to do unimaginable things.

As soon as Pete noticed what Falcort was doing, he tried to strengthen the barrier that blocked King Falcort from entering, but it was too late. Out of the black clouds protruded long thin strands of the cloud that seemed to be like an arm. The arms that had protruded struck the outer barrier with such force that a shock wave was sent all the way through the sky and across the grounds where the barrier had descended to. The arm-like clouds began to twist and turn and attack the barrier like small horizontal tornados.

As the cloud tore at the barrier, Pete began to get the six armies into their positions, ready for anything that was about to come. The blue, silver, and brown armies went to the front for open battle while the rest stayed back to protect the colony and attack with greater force.

Archers lined the rooftops, just like when they arrived. The Flight Warriors and Teleporters lined the outside of the castle walls, ready to attack at any moment.

When the arm-like clouds finally broke through the barrier, the force field was lifted from around the grounds from all angles. There was no more protection. It was open battle now. The black clouds flooded the sky until they hit the shining light beam that was protruded from the green eye in the sky. They circled around the eye until everything was dark except for around the colony. The small light that did shine in still lit up the entire grounds; it just wasn't as bright.

As the clouds circled the grounds, King Falcort had raised his hands into the air that held his wand. He began to recite the enchantments that would awaken his army:

"Warriors of night, awaken now and fight for your kingdom. The dead of mutants and wizards rise from the world's dirt and travel here now, come to fight as warriors. Be reborn for your last time, for this one battle. Take control and only bring me triumph."

After he spoke the simple but difficult enchantment, he began to talk in a different language known only to magical creatures, cursing them.

After King Falcort spoke his words of war to his warriors, the forests that surrounded the castle stirred with magical creatures, and the creatures ran out to fight for their new master. All the animals' eyes glowed red as they ran toward the courts' armies to be the first to attack. This was one of Falcort's flaws. Above where Falcort stood, a red bolt of energy shot out of his wand and exploded in the sky to reveal a red eye just like the one Pete had created.

Pete knew that Falcort had better armies than just a bunch of magical creatures. He feared that King Falcort had awakened the dead to come to fight for him. And soon his fear came true.

Across the oceans that surrounded the school's location flew black specks of smoke. The smoke flew into the dark black clouds and circled inside of them and then shot out toward the ground from the large red eye.

The smoke turned into red jets of light as they shot out from the eye. They struck the ground, and soon after they had struck, man-sized skeletons with little flesh erupted from the dirt and began running toward the courts' armies. Each had either a short wooden wand, which looked dead because the leaf buds around them were brown and lifeless, or a mutant power.

The ones with the wands were dead witches and wizards who had been reborn with their same magical abilities. The mutants had their mutant power as well. The reborn people didn't look human at all. They all had torn faces and wore ragged robes.

Awakening the dead only allowed their bodies to return. Their souls and minds moved on. The curse that gave them new life was terrible. Only a few wizards had used the curse. King Falcort was one who thought the curse was very useful. He didn't care about its consequences of fear and miserable things that came when using it. The awakening curse gave the bodies of the dead function and movement and also a mindset of whatever the awakener wanted them to do for him.

The reborn people ran across the large grounds, attacking with all they could. Unsteady spells and curses shot at the courts' warriors, hitting only some. The armies were awaiting their clue of when to attack. The magical creatures were not that much ahead of the dead but were gaining ground.

"Archers, arm your weapons!" Pete screamed. "Aim," Pete ordered aloud. And as he yelled out, "Fire!" the golden arrows shot out from the gifted archers and raced across the sky. The jinxed arrows gained speed as they began to glow bright gold. The arrows all seemed to create their own wind as they traced across the sky. When they struck the objects they hit, the objects exploded and turned into dust. Some of the arrows hit the ground, creating craters and causing some of King Falcort's army to fall in the newly made holes. The arrows had struck a lot of Falcort's army, but the army wasn't weakened nearly enough.

Red bolts of light kept flying down into the ground, creating new walking dead people. King Falcort's army's numbers soon grew to double. The courts were doomed in Falcort's eyes, but the courts had well-trained and very skilled warriors that still matched Falcort's army even if it was five times the size of the courts' army.

"Attack!" Pete finally yelled out to his fellow warriors.

The warriors who lined the front ran toward the enemy's armies with much greater speed than the dead walking people. Swords and spears began slashing, and wands began flicking as the two armies fought. The magical creatures were wiped out right away by the front line and stood no chance. When the two armies met, the green eye that was up in the sky raged with fire as it shot out a green wave that dissolved the dark clouds that were overhead the courts' armies.

As the battle went on, the courts had taken out a lot of Falcort's army but were badly weakened. Falcort's army was still growing, and the courts' powers were diminishing.

More images flashed before Pete as he grew more knowledgeable of the war. After the images flashed before him, he came upon something very familiar—a memory.. He soon stood in the same room he ended up in the night he discovered the necklace. And in front of him was his father, sitting in the chair, staring not at Pete but still talking to him.

Chapter Thirty-Two

"You have entered the war, and there is no turning back. You have full control of your power and must call to the heavens for your army. You must call to the Angel Warriors who await their chance to fight. This is the last of my appearances as a memory. I wish you good luck," George finished while the green haze swirled and eventually vanished.

Pete stood back in front of the ongoing battle. The courts were still losing strength, and King Falcort's army was still growing.

As Pete watched, new knowledge came to him, and, like all the other times, he had no idea how it had come. Pete slashed his wand up into the air and pointed it at the green eye that raged in line with the sun. He began to glow green, and so did the wand. As he glowed, a golden substance circled his body and began to coil around the wand. The shape of a dragon's neck and head formed until the mouth of the dragon opened and the golden substance shot out of it up toward the green eye.

The green around the eye exploded and caused it to glow all the colors of the courts except red. Light beams shot from the color-filled eye and struck the battleground. The light beams acted as gateways for the Angel Warriors to enter the battle.

Figures dressed in white ran, flew, and jumped out of the light gateways and immediately formed a line in front of the other courts' armies. The Angel Warriors defeated the walking dead people that were behind the frontline, and the walking dead people had to get through the frontline to get any closer to winning the battle.

Falcort's army backed off away from the frontline because the glow coming from the Angel Warriors stunted the walking dead people. It was some kind of spell that kept them away.

As more Angel Warriors poured out of the gateways, dragons with golden armor and lions flew and ran out of the gateways.

As the new army came into action, Pete had a new piece of knowledge come to him that was very important. King Falcort had the serpent king on his side, also known to some as the devil. There was a spell that could open the doors to hell if conjured. The only way Falcort could conjure this spell was with a life sacrifice.

Whose life will be sacrificed? Pete wondered. And that's when he sensed it. King Falcort had someone whom Pete had grown to be very close to during his little time at school. He sensed that Lucy was in trouble.

CHAPTER THIRTY-THREE

Alongside the mountain where King Falcort was, along with his vast amount of followers, Lucy was tied up in a chair. She couldn't scream because she was gagged.

"It's almost time. The weak one has sent the army from the heavens," Falcort said, seeming as if he had the war already won and that the courts stood no chance.

The red eye still shot out red beams, creating walking dead people, and the black clouds still stood even though the light from the green eye diminished most of them. After the rest of the Angel Warriors arrived, the red color-filled eye and the black clouds got thicker and covered most of the grounds again. Falcort was responding with full force now.

"It's time. Bring me the girl," Falcort ordered two of his followers.

They brought Lucy up to the spot where Falcort stood. Falcort grabbed Lucy by the hair and pulled her head down to show the back of her neck. Lucy whimpered.

"Let us see your true power, little missy," Falcort said sarcastically.

Falcort took out his wand and stabbed the tip of it into the back of Lucy's neck. The end of the snake's mouth on the wand dug into Lucy's skin and formed a burn mark in the shape of a black, curvy F.

Falcort ripped the cloth from around Lucy's mouth as she let out the most terrible scream. Her eyes turned dark red and her skin darkened as she screamed. Falcort flicked his wand at her as he controlled what she did with his mind.

Lucy put her hands down to her sides as she rose up into the air. The clouds darkened even more and covered the entire grounds except around the green eye. Lightning flashed, thunder roared, and the wind picked up as she went higher into the air. Red lightning flashed as tornadoes formed and began attacking the Angel Warriors and the court armies.

Back to where Pete and the leaders of the six courts stood, Queen Issia stepped out from the line they had made and said nervously, "Oh no, Luciana! That's my daughter."

Before anyone could stop her, she too flew up into the air; she went to try to help her daughter. As she got close, Lucy sent bolts of red lightning at her mother. Queen Issia stopped the attack with bolts of her own lightning that blocked Lucy's from hitting her.

"Luciana, don't listen to him. Come to me. Let me help you. He's going to kill you!" Queen Issia yelled over the loud thunder that roared.

Lucy realized that it was her mother. She began to weaken the storm she had made, but Falcort gave her an order to kill Queen Issia. It wasn't working though.

"She knows it's her mother. She doesn't want to hurt her," Falcort said out loud with anger.

Falcort raised his wand at Queen Issia and screamed as a red bolt of light struck Queen Issia, causing her to fall.

"No!" Pete yelled aloud from across the grounds. As he said it, he conjured a force field that acted like a blanket to soften the queen's fall. He could barely see her, but she landed softly and did not move, though.

"Kill all of them," King Falcort ordered Lucy through mind control while flicking his wand toward her.

The weak control Lucy had over her power was totally taken from her, and she went out of control. The black clouds swooped down closer to where the court's armies were, along with the Angel Warriors, and began to pour acid rain.

The acid rain began eating at all of the warrior's armor and skin; they began to fall to the ground to their deaths. The Land Warriors weren't affected as much by the rain, and they started to jump into the dirt below them. As each Land Warrior sank into the ground, a large tree sprouted and grew to be as large as a redwood tree. These trees' branches spread out into a hundred-foot diameter and created a canopy to protect all the other warriors from the rain.

Falcort raged with anger and had Lucy send tornadoes upon the newly made trees. Tornados swept down upon the trees and began tearing them apart, killing warriors at the same time.

Pete had had enough of King Falcort's attacks. He was ready to end this battle. Pete leapt from where he was standing and flew through the air toward Lucy. He was flying as fast as he could, but when he reached her, he hadn't been fast enough to save her. Lucy's nonmoving body fell from the sky, just like her mother, but this time Pete had caught her and set her down by her mother. The storm Lucy created stopped, and Pete watched to make sure she wasn't dead, but he thought for sure she was. As he sat, the walking dead people started running toward him, but before they reached him, the red eye that was suspended among the clouds above, where King Falcort stood, screeched and sent a large beam of red light into the water.

Pete sat there, amazed at what he was seeing. A large whirlpool formed where the beam hit and drained all the water from the sea. As the final water went down the hole, there was a loud cracking noise as a small castle-shaped structure formed and shot red-hot lava everywhere like the top of an erupting volcano. The walking dead people turned to dust as the castle shot out of the ground. Pete knew from the book what this was—it wasn't good.

Chapter Thirty-Four

The castle held the doors to hell, which would unleash terrible monsters in the world. These monsters fed on human flesh and could eat thousands before they became satisfied but would soon repeat the feeding frenzy on humans. Falcort's army was unstoppable, at least that was what many highly ranked wizards and mutants believed. Falcort would be able to control the world finally if hell's doors were opened. The only way to stop the doors from being opened would be to destroy the castle, or at least damage it, and kill King Falcort before he could summon hell's army. The castle walls were at their weakest before the summoning, which would be the time to attack.

Pete stood up from kneeling down by Lucy, and as he stood, Lucy's body vanished into red flames. King Falcort had summoned her body and was ready to summon hell's army. Pete grabbed a hold of Queen Issia, and with a green flash they vanished and appeared in line with the five courts' leaders who were still in line.

"Take her inside into the teleporting room in the east wing. Get everybody out of here. I'm the only one who can finish this battle," Pete ordered the five court leaders.

The five court leaders began to oppose Pete's decision, but Pete didn't listen; he instead was trying to find where Ben and Miguel had gone. He soon found Miguel; he was running toward Pete, breathing hard.

"Pete, it's Ben. He just vanished for no reason. He was trying to find a way to attack Falcort and kill him, and he was talking to me and vanished," Miguel finished while still breathing hard. "Before he vanished, I saw King Falcort's mark on the back of his neck. I think Falcort must have summoned him," Miguel finished.

"Get everyone out of here. I must go now," Pete ordered Miguel.

"No, I'm coming with you," Miguel argued back at Pete.

Just as Miguel spoke, Pete vanished and appeared in front of the castle where its doors were opened. Pete started toward the doors and noticed guards at the doors. Pete slashed his hands in the guards' directions, and the two guards immediately fell to the ground, unconscious.

Pete walked into the castle and entered a large room that seemed to be the entire castle, which was lined with black brick. In the center of the room was a huge, black stone that stuck out of the floor, and hanging from the side of it was Lucy. Her hands and feet were tied to the rock. King Falcort had started the summoning but would soon be interrupted.

Pete pulled out his wand, grasped it with one hand on each side, and pulled his fists apart away from the ends of the wand, causing the wand to turn into a brown-black-greenish smoke formation. The smoke formation encased around his hands and formed small, round smoke formations at his palms.

Pete yelled while clapping his hands together, "Stop!" and as his hands touched each other, there was a green spark and a thick force field erupted from around him, crashing into the blackened brick walls.

The doorway behind him blasted apart, creating an even larger hole in the wall. The sidewalls cracked, and smaller holes formed. Half the ceiling fell to the ground behind Pete, and the castle had enough damage to postpone the summoning.

"You will not be opening the doors today or any other day. This war is over!" Pete yelled to Falcort, standing in front of Lucy.

To Pete's surprise, Falcort seemed to be the only one in the castle. All of his followers must have still been along the mountainside.

Falcort turned toward Pete and spoke very sharply, "The war is far from over, and I will open the doors to hell."

King Falcort whipped his wand from his side and said something Pete didn't understand, but common sense told him it was some kind of dark magic curse. The red beam shot at Pete like a bullet, but Pete stopped it from hitting him with the curse Rebbelo. The two smoke balls shot out green jets of light.

As the two curses made contact, a ball of energy formed, sending shocks around the room. Pete's eyes began to glow green, and Falcort's entire body was engulfed in red flames. From the corner of the room, Ben stood, chained up.

"You must stab him with the golden sword. Stab him in the necklace," Ben yelled but was stopped by someone Pete hadn't seen when he walked in. He didn't see Ben there either. Whoever it was took Ben with them in a flash of yellow light.

Pete disconnected the bond between the curses and sent a wave of energy up into one of the large beams that held the ceiling up. A large piece of the beam broke apart, and Pete sent it toward Falcort. He saw it coming and shot a spark of yellow light at it, causing the beam to split in two. Falcort raised his hands encased around his wand into the air, making the beam connect back together and shoot back toward Pete, who stopped the beam by turning it into dust.

King Falcort began shooting the same dark magic curse and all other stunning spells at Pete as fast as he could. Pete dodged them all but dodged some just barely. Pete, after just missing one of Falcort's curses, began to shoot spells at Falcort, missing him too. The amount of force Pete's spells had was a lot more than Falcort's. Finally one of Pete's stunning spells hit Falcort, causing his wand to fly out of his hand, slamming him to the ground.

Chapter Thirty-Five

As King Falcort fell to the ground, stunned, Pete clapped his hands together, causing another force field to go through the air, which covered the inside of the entire room. After he produced the force field, the balls of smoke turned back into his wand. The force field was different; it sort of thickened the air. It was the immobilizing force field. No magic could fly through the room now unless performed by Pete.

Pete was right about seeing the necklace around Falcort's neck back at Ben's cabin. Ben didn't believe him, but now he did all of a sudden. It must be because Ben saw the necklace himself now. Falcort looked much older than he did fifteen years ago when he was brought back to life. Wrinkles were etched upon his face like a web. The wrinkles stained black with what looked like ashes.

The red-eyed necklace was worn around Falcort's neck and seemed to have no damage to it. It must still have power. And if it did, then why didn't Falcort use it on Pete? The reason was about to be explained to Pete by King Falcort himself.

"You win, I suppose. This isn't the first time I have been defeated," King Falcort said in a confident voice. "But it shall be my last defeat," Falcort said while laughing.

"You're right. It will be your last. You won't ever have to be defeated again because after I leave here, you will never exist again," Pete said to Falcort while walking toward him.

As Pete got closer to Falcort, he sensed its power. The power was encased though; it wouldn't work. When Pete was just a few yards away from his enemy, the red-eyed necklace revealed its past to Pete. It revealed everything Falcort had done. As the necklace revealed its past, time seemed to stop.

Flashes of red light shot through Pete's mind as he saw human figures fall to their deaths. A war scene came into play as Pete watched as Falcort fought alongside Ben against huge creatures that were attacking them. Then Pete ended up in a room, watching his father talking to Falcort. The only words he heard his father say were: "Just show my successor the truth, and I shall spare your life."

The memory twisted as images of a storm rolling in through the sky circled a house, just like where Pete lived with his mother. A flash of red light shown as he saw his father fall to the ground dead, his mother in pain, pregnant with him. There was a tall man with dark hair who was stirring something in a small flask. A blast of white light shined, and a man came from the center. An image of two babies came into view. Images of buildings falling and bridges collapsing traced through his mind. And finally an image of Pete showed up with his eyes glowing red.

Pete came back to his normal state, and time started again. Falcort still lay on the ground, stunned, and Pete stood in front of him, looking straight into his eyes. Falcort smiled while seeing Pete's expression.

"You killed my father?" Pete asked angrily.

"Yes, it was under my orders to have him killed," Falcort answered calmly.

"Why? What did he ever do to you?" Pete questioned.

"He did nothing except try to control me," Falcort replied, trying to get up.

Pete strengthened the stunning spell so Falcort couldn't move. "Who wouldn't want to control you? All you do is kill people!" Pete shouted.

"You saw the memory didn't you? The one about me telling the truth to George's successor?" Falcort asked Pete.

"Yes," Pete replied calmer. "And you're going to tell me everything you know. There are things I have seen that I need answers to," Pete finished.

"It all started back when George started running the courts. The war began, and the courts fell apart. He had no more control. The war was just like now, six courts against one. He wanted to gather the courts back together. He wanted peace. I had discovered magic he didn't even know of. That's when he got controlling. The magical bind placed between the courts and George allowed him to control what we could do with the magic inside our necklaces." Falcort paused, trying to move again, but couldn't budge.

Pete saw figures gathering outside the barrier he created. He knew something was about to happen.

"I gained too much power for him, and he banished me. He took my powers. Then we met for a meeting, at his request. He told me that I must tell his successor everything that had gone on, or I would never see life again. When my powers were taken, I became weak. I began to die with every magical act. George did not know this. My followers scattered, and the war ended at that time. As I suffered, a helper showed up to assist me. I was reborn." Falcort paused again.

"Why are you telling me all of this? Isn't the villain only supposed to say enough to get what he wants when he's under pressure?" Pete said sarcastically.

"Yes, but I haven't said enough yet. I was reborn by your mother's blood the night I had your father killed. And that is when the green-eyed necklace was possible to retrieve. Your mother gave me life, but I couldn't get the necklace unless I cursed your father's offspring to be someone else. And in that case I cursed the baby inside your mother to be equal to me. It allowed me to have a lot of plans, but the first failed. The necklace wasn't possible to retrieve. I was weakened by cursing the unborn baby and had to wait." Falcort stopped for a second.

Pete sat, listening closely, deciphering what Falcort was saying. Things from the book fell into place as Falcort explained the past.

"And after I waited, I discovered that the cursed baby would have to find the necklace first." Falcort paused. "And here you are now. You have found the necklace, and its power belongs to both of us," Falcort finished.

"No, the power only belongs to my family. I will not allow you to trick me into letting you have the power," Pete said firmly.

"Don't you see? Your mother has been lying to you all your life. She hasn't told you about the necklace, your father, and about the night I cursed the baby inside her," Falcort said loudly.

Pete grasped his wand as the end where the dragon's neck coiled around split apart and a golden blade protruded out from it. The wand turned into the handle of the golden sword.

"What are you doing?" Falcort asked.

"Doing what my father should have done. You bent the way my father intended your life to go from when he took your powers. He wanted you to find good in yourself. Instead he died for the jealously over power you had, and you're trying to trick me into giving you the power of my necklace," Pete said while pointing the sword at Falcort.

"You have misunderstood. I have told you the truth, which means I have the right to life. Which was your father's intention," Falcort said in a fake, pleading voice, but Pete didn't catch the fakeness in it.

"You twisted magic, and the curse my father put on you was overturned. I have learned lots of magic in little time, but I know the curse used on you from my mother's blood. You could die any time now, and it doesn't matter what my father's intentions were. The only intention I have now is to rid you of this world and all other worlds forever," Pete said in a confident voice.

"Yes, you are correct—" Falcort began.

Pete pointed his open hand at Falcort and caused him to rise into the air, stopping him. Pete began to glow green as Falcort glowed red also.

"I take the power vested in me and the seven courts, and I rid you along with your use of power from the courts forever, and I take your life as the sacrifice," Pete said while pushing the tip of the sword into the red-eyed necklace and through Falcort's chest.

The red-eyed necklace split in two as the power Falcort had gained was lost. Pete stopped glowing, but red flames raged around Falcort as he spoke his final words, "You have it all wrong. You will regret this. This is only the beginning."

Pete pulled the sword out of Falcort's chest as Falcort began to shine bright red and blasted apart into dust. The necklace fell to the ground, and only a cloud of blackness remained.

CHAPTER THIRTY-SIX

The force field that surrounded him distorted as the people Pete thought he saw vanished. The golden sword turned back into his wand, and Pete felt a sudden loss of strength, but soon it came back to him. He went to grab the red-eyed necklace, but as he went to pick it up, he saw a shadow flash red across the walls and was hit by something.

Pete flew back onto the ground not far from the necklace and could not move. A hooded individual came in front of him and took off his hood. The person Pete saw was someone who looked just like him. He sounded like him also but talked with a subtle difference.

"You should have listened to him. He was right. This is only the beginning."

The boy who looked like Pete, Franklin, picked up the red-eyed necklace and put it on. The necklace glowed, along with Franklin's body, as the necklace was put back together.

The boy vanished; the ground began to shake as the castle walls fell down upon where Pete lay. The sky got light again as the red eye disappeared and all of the walking dead people vanished. The human followers of Falcort vanished as well, and everything became calm.

All Pete could see was the walls crashing down on him until he felt his strength come back. He stood up and created a cocoon force field that protected him from the falling walls. The walls of the castle turned to dust and fell flat to the ground until Pete was looking around outside. The castle walls had turned to dust before hitting Lucy, leaving her untouched.

Soon after the castle fell, Franklin appeared in the same spot he vanished from with his skin stained with black ashes that flaked off his skin like they were scales on a fish. And at that moment, they both encountered a feeling that was not ordinary, and neither would know what it was for some time. The feeling felt like they were light headed. And as they felt it, the air in between them formed ripples as if there was some sort of force field that was created without either one doing so. They both noticed but hardly paid attention and looked back at each other.

"I told you, you would regret killing me." Franklin's skin had flakes of ashes, putting his flesh back into original state, and he did not speak in the same voice he had before but in King Falcort's voice, and he vanished once again.

To be continued …